D0424047

Dear Reader,

This book marks the end of another trilogy. I'm not sure why these sexy men always seem to find me in groups of three, but they do. I'm sure there's another trio waiting right around the corner to hop onto the pages of my next three books.

Readers often ask where I get my ideas. Thankfully, there's never a shortage of inspiration. The world is full of bad boys—Charmers and Drifters and Sexy Devils—all just waiting for their own story and their own heroine to introduce them to the power of love.

I hope you've enjoyed reading the Smooth Operators trilogy as much as I've enjoyed writing it.

Happy reading,

Kate Hoffmann

Kate Hoffmann

THE SEXY DEVIL

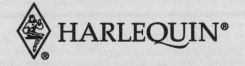

TORONTO • NEW YORK • LONDON
AMSTERDAM • PARIS • SYDNEY • HAMBURG
STOCKHOLM • ATHENS • TOKYO • MILAN • MADRID
PRAGUE • WARSAW • BUDAPEST • AUCKLAND

Recycling programs
for this product may
not exist in your area.

ISBN-13: 978-0-373-79550-5

THE SEXY DEVIL

Copyright © 2010 by Peggy A. Hoffmann.

This edition published by arrangement with Harlequin Books S.A.

For questions and comments about the quality of this book
please contact us at Customer_eCare@Harlequin.ca.

® and TM are trademarks of the publisher. Trademarks indicated with ® are registered in the United States Patent and Trademark Office, the Canadian Trade Marks Office and in other countries.

www.eHarlequin.com

Printed in U.S.A.

ABOUT THE AUTHOR

Kate Hoffmann began writing for Harlequin Books in 1993. Since then she's published sixty books, primarily in the Harlequin Temptation and Harlequin Blaze lines. When she isn't writing, she enjoys music, theater and musical theater. She is active, working with high school students in the performing arts. She lives in southeastern Wisconsin with her two cats, Chloe and Tally.

Books by Kate Hoffmann

1

"ALEXANDER NIKOLAS STAMOS of Chicago and Tenley Jacinda Marshall of Sawyer Bay, Wisconsin, were married on Saturday in a traditional ceremony at St. Andrew's Greek Orthodox Church. Stamos, president and CEO of Stamos Publishing, and his bride will reside in Lincoln Park after a honeymoon in Tahiti." Celia Peralto leaned back in her chair and sighed. "So they're going to live happily ever after."

Angela Weatherby glanced over her shoulder. "Alex Stamos was the exception to the rule," she said softly. "He's an aberration, part of the margin of error."

"And what about Charlie Templeton?" Ceci asked. "He's getting married, too."

"He's engaged. He's not married yet," Angela said stubbornly. She spun to face Ceci, her hands clutching the arms of her desk chair. "Listen, this isn't doing me any good. Every time this happens, I start to doubt the thesis of my book. Please, can you just keep these stories to yourself until I finish?"

This book was turning into a nightmare. Every time Angela thought she had her thesis nailed, something came along to screw it all up. She just needed to be right about this. These men—these smooth operators—weren't supposed to change. They weren't supposed to fall in love and get married and live happily ever after.

She hadn't set out to write a book about bad boys and the women who loved them. With her career as a freelance writer stalled, Angela had begun writing a blog, ruminating on the state of the male-female dynamic in contemporary dating. After hundreds of women had begun relating their own dating disaster stories, the blog had turned into a Web site, filled with profiles of thousands of men and a catalog of their dating atrocities. And now, Angela was about to put all of her theories and research into a book, *Smooth Operators: A Woman's Guide to Avoiding Dating Disasters.*

"Ever since you've started this book, you've been really tense," Ceci said.

"I should be tense. It was due at the publisher three months ago and I can't seem to finish."

"Maybe you should put it down for a while and reconsider your reasons for writing it."

"I know what you think," Angela said. "And I'm not doing this because I want to prove something to my parents."

"Oh, really?" Ceci asked. "Both your parents are psychologists who've written numerous books. They both teach at prestigious universities here in Chicago. Your older sister is a neurosurgeon and your younger sister is a physicist. This is your chance to step up to the Weatherby plate and hit a home run."

"A baseball metaphor?" Angela asked. Her thoughts shifted, an image of a handsome man flashing in her mind. Max Morgan. Professional baseball player. Classic smooth operator. And the subject of Chapter Five—the Sexy Devil.

"Sorry," Ceci said. "It's all Will can talk about. Baseball, baseball, baseball. He's in this ridiculous fantasy league and they get together every Monday night at some bar over in DePaul. I have no idea what they do, but he can't stop talking about it."

Angela turned back to her computer. Max Morgan. For such a long time, she'd barely thought of him. And then, one day, she'd been looking at profiles on the site and there he was. Twenty-six women had commented on him, and the comments were far from flattering. Since then, she couldn't keep from wondering what had turned her teenage Prince Charming into one of her bad-boy archetypes.

Throughout her childhood, Angela tried her best to please her parents, cultivating a rational and practical facade. But inside, Angela knew she wasn't like her sisters. They dreamed of academic glory while she secretly dreamed of romance and adventure, of being rescued from her dull existence by a white knight with a heart of gold.

As a young girl, she'd waited, secretly smuggling romantic novels into her backpack at the library—*Jane Eyre, Pride and Prejudice, Gone with the Wind.* As she devoured each one, she became the heroine, strong and feisty, the kind of girl every man wanted for his own.

And on the day she began high school, she'd met the man of her dreams, her prince, her white knight—Max Morgan. They'd bumped into each other in the registration line and from that moment on, Angela knew they were meant to be together. He'd been tall and beautiful, with chocolate-brown eyes and a mop of unruly, sun-streaked hair.

He'd said one word to her—"sorry"—and she'd fallen deeply and madly in love, or at least as deeply as a fifteen-year-old could. He'd never noticed her again. Forget about Mr. Rochester, Mr. Darcy and Rhett Butler. Max Morgan became the stuff of all her secret fantasies.

She'd followed him around high school, secretly watching everything he did. She attended his football games and baseball games, describing every moment in her diary in great detail so that she could relive it all over again when she was alone.

When it came time for college, she made a last minute decision to go to Northwestern in her home-town of Evanston, rather than an Ivy League school as her parents had wanted. Her self-respect denied that the only reason for the change was because Max had decided on Northwestern, securing both a football and baseball scholarship his freshman year.

"Hope springs eternal," Ceci said in a cheery voice. "It does give you hope, doesn't it? That maybe the men you've written off as…unsalvageable might just need the right woman?"

"No!" Angela said. "Our Web site proves my point every day. SmoothOperators has thousands of profiles of men who can't commit."

She couldn't be wrong. This was her one chance to prove to her parents that she wasn't wasting her time with this "silly Web site" as they called it. She saw it as a giant petri dish, a source of ever-evolving information about how men and women related in the world of dating. Her undergrad degree in psychology and her graduate degree in journalism made her the perfect person to write this book.

Ceci sighed. "I bet they both had a moment. Now, that would make good material for a book."

"Who? What are you talking about?"

Ceci rolled her chair over to Angela's desk. "Charlie Templeton and Alex Stamos. They had a moment and they were magically transformed into decent guys."

Angela rolled her eyes and shook her head. "There's nothing magical about this. They probably just decided they were tired of playing the field. The instinct to procreate kicked in. Once they've done that, they'll dump the wife and hit the bars again."

"I don't think so. Look at how fast it happened for them. They had a moment. You know, that instant when your eyes meet and you realize your life is about to change forever and there's nothing you can do about it. Maybe that deserves a chapter in your book. Chapter Fourteen. The Moment."

Though she didn't want to admit it, Angela knew exactly what Ceci was talking about. She'd experienced a moment…once, about four years ago. But it hadn't changed her life. "Have you ever had a moment?" Angela asked, keeping her gaze fixed on her work.

"No," Ceci admitted.

"Not even with Will?"

"Nope. It might happen, though. It doesn't have to be the moment you meet. That's love at first sight. For some people, it happens a little later. And sometimes it happens at different times for men and women. My brother-in-law said he fell in love with my sister when she burned a pot roast for his birthday dinner. She sat on the kitchen floor and cried for a half hour. And that was the moment he knew they'd be together forever."

Unfortunately, it had taken Angela six years to realize that she and Max would never have a moment. She'd even wrangled an interview with him for the college paper, but she'd been so nervous, she could barely remember the questions she'd planned to ask. After that, they'd passed each other on campus on numerous occasions, and even shared a sociology class. But he'd never once given her a second glance.

The summer after her sophomore year, Angela set out to transform herself into the kind of girl Max would notice. She studied the fashion magazines and bought a whole new wardrobe. She dyed her mousy brown hair a pretty shade of honey-blonde. She got herself a pair of contacts and lost ten pounds. She silently observed the girls that Max found attractive and she turned herself into one, then waited for her moment, determined to turn it into something special.

But it wasn't to be. At the end of his sophomore baseball season, Max left college for the minor leagues, signing with the Tampa Bay Devil Rays. He packed his bags and headed south for their farm system.

She knew her last chance at romance was gone, so she'd done exactly what the rational middle daughter of the Doctors Weatherby should do—she moved on. She started dating other guys and within a year, Max Morgan had become a distant memory from an all-too-foolish adolescence.

Until that night, four years ago. A night that could have changed the course of her life—except it hadn't. "There was a moment," Angela murmured. "With this one guy."

Ceci leaned forward. "Really? With who?"

"With whom," Angela corrected.

"With whom!" Ceci said.

"I was out with a coworker at a sports bar in Evanston. I came there to meet her cousin, a stockbroker. It was a blind date. Our eyes met across the bar and it was like I'd been struck by lightning. It took my breath away. We stared at each other for what seemed like forever. It was…frightening and exhilarating. And I felt like I was under some kind of…I don't know. Spell."

"See! You know exactly what I'm talking about! What happened?"

"Nothing. I got nervous and looked away. When I looked back, some other woman had captured his attention."

"But this guy was your blind date," Ceci said. "God, what a creep. He went off with another girl?"

"No!" Angela said. "My blind date was sitting next to me, rattling on about bond rates and investment strategies. This was a different guy."

It was the only real regret she had in her life. She'd let her one last chance at Max Morgan slip away. As his career in the majors blossomed that season, he became the stuff of tabloid legend, slowly transforming himself into her archetypical smooth operator—dating a long string of models and actresses and party girls, then tossing them aside when something more interesting came along.

Angela had gone home that night and wrote her first blog, talking about what she called "White Knight Syndrome," and her silly dream of finding the perfect man to rescue her from the horrors of single life.

Ceci reached out and took Angela's hand. "That's so tragic."

Angela shook her head, lost in thoughts of Max. "No, it isn't," she said stubbornly. "It wasn't meant to be. If he'd been interested, he would have walked across that bar and introduced himself."

"And you'd be married to him today," Ceci said.

"No!" Angela protested. "We might have gone out, had a nice time, maybe slept together, but then he would have turned out to be like all the others."

"You don't know that," Ceci said.

"I do." Angela paused, not sure of how much she wanted to reveal to Ceci. "He has a huge profile on our site. Nearly fifty women have commented. I would have been just another in a long line of broken hearts."

"You found him on the site?"

"Actually, he's the reason I started the blog," Angela admitted. "We went to high school and college together and I had this massive crush on him. He never noticed me. We had that moment in the bar and I realized what a ridiculous fool I was, still carrying a torch for him after all those years. That night, I went home and wrote my first blog."

"What's his name?" Ceci asked, turning back to her computer. "I want to look him up." She clicked on the search engine, then waited.

Why not tell Ceci? It's not like she had feelings for

him anymore. "He's the Sexy Devil," she murmured. "Chapter Five. Max Morgan."

Ceci's hands froze on her keyboard and she slowly turned to face Angela. "You know Max Morgan? The baseball player?" She sighed in frustration. "How many times have we talked about him? About his chapter in the book. And you never told me you knew him."

"I don't, exactly." Angela shrugged. "I've spoken to him…once. No, twice if you count the one word he said to me when we first met. I know almost everything there is to know about him. But we don't know each other. He's not even aware I exist."

"But you had a moment!" Ceci cried. "Maybe you were destined for each other."

"Love is not about magic moments and fairy-tale endings," Angela said. "It's about two people willing to work hard to make a relationship succeed. Two people sharing common interests and goals. And there are few truly decent men around willing to invest the time and effort to make a relationship work."

"You sound just like your mother," Ceci said. "So what are you going to do? Are you going to interview him?" She frowned. "Wait a second. Is that why you didn't go to that big charity event? The one he was hosting last month?"

"It wouldn't have been a good place to conduct an interview. I have to get him alone and talking, without any distractions." She swallowed hard. "And

I'm not sure I want to catch him. I have several other candidates for that chapter."

In truth, Angela had thought an interview would be the perfect opportunity to prove to herself that her feelings for Max Morgan were gone for good. She was adult now and she'd put all her teenage fantasies about love behind her. He wasn't her Prince Charming. Max Morgan was just another serial seducer, bent on bolstering his ego with an endless supply of willing women. It wouldn't take more than a few minutes in his presence to recognize that he was not the man of her dreams.

"I think the reason you made him the subject of Chapter Five is because you want to see him again," Ceci said. "You had a moment and you can't forget it. And don't bother lying to me. I'm your best friend. Whenever you lie, your face turns red."

Angela clapped her hands over her cheeks and shook her head. "I'll interview him. But my luck with interviews has been pretty bad lately. I can't help it if no one wants to talk to me."

"What if I could set you up with Max Morgan?" Ceci said.

"How would you do that?"

"Will hangs out at the Tenth Inning every Monday night with his fantasy league buddies. Max Morgan owns the Tenth Inning. And Will says that Max has been in occasionally these last few weeks. He's back in Chicago for the summer, recuperating after some sort of surgery he had during the off-season."

"How do you know all this?"

"Occasionally, I do listen to Will's rambling. He even met Max last week. Got a photo of him on his phone. I'm sure if you went in there, you could talk to him."

Angela felt her stomach flutter and she drew a sharp breath, pushing the surge of excitement aside. Ceci was right. She shouldn't be afraid to interview Max. She could certainly maintain a professional demeanor, even taking into account her former feelings about him.

"If I'm going to interview him, we have to develop a better strategy. He can't know he's being interviewed. I have to find a way to meet him and then get whatever I need from casual conversation." Angela stood. "He can't know that this is for a book."

"Conversation," Ceci said. "That's exactly what people do in a bar."

"I know. But I've never been very good at that. I don't flirt, I have a tendency to babble when I'm nervous, and I absolutely cannot hold my liquor."

"That's the least of your problems," Ceci said. "First, we have to go shopping and buy you the sexiest outfit on the planet. You're going to have to attract him first. From what I see on his profile, he doesn't have any shortage of women wanting to sleep with him. What do you think—legs, belly or cleavage? Pick one."

"For what?"

"It's my mother's rule. She always used to tell me

that if your outfit only showed one of the three, it was sexy. Two of the three makes the outfit sleazy. And showing all three makes it slutty. The rule of three has served me well. So, legs, belly or boobs?"

"What do you think?" Angela asked, staring down at her rather unremarkable body.

"Legs," Ceci said. "You have great legs. Let him fantasize about the boobs and the belly." Ceci grabbed her purse, then pulled Angela along toward the door. "What color?"

"Does your mom have a rule for that as well?"

"No. I do. Black is boring, red is desperate. An unusual color, like chartreuse or tangerine, says you're a strong, independent woman who doesn't care what other people say about her weird color choices. And men think that women who wear weird colors are kinky in bed."

"You have proof of this?" Angela asked.

"Yes." She pointed to her own mustard-colored top. "I was wearing pumpkin-orange when I met Will. He said he knew exactly what I was like in the bedroom."

"I'm not going to sleep with Max Morgan," Angela said.

"Of course not. But in order to get close to him, you're going to have to make him believe you just might."

They stepped out of the office onto the noisy bustle of Ashland Avenue. It was barely noon and the heat was already stifling. "There's this really nice boutique that just opened on North," Ceci said. "Let's start there. You'll need a nice pair of Do-me shoes, too. The dress will be demure but the shoes will say 'take my body now'."

"You are not my fairy godmother and I'm not Cinderella."

Ceci slipped her arm through Angela's. "Honey, we all want to be Cinderella. Every single girl I know is waiting for that guy to come calling with a glass slipper."

THE BAR WAS CROWDED for a Tuesday night. Max Morgan leaned over and motioned to Dave, his manager and big brother. "Is this a typical Tuesday night? This is the busiest I've seen it in ages. What's going on?"

"It's Ladies' Night. Women drink for half-price on Tuesdays. And when you're here, a lot of women show up, hoping they'll get lucky," Dave said, grinning. "Hey, you're better than a promotional giveaway. The women want to date you, the men want to talk baseball with you. Just sit yourself down at the end of the bar and be your usual charming self. Or better yet, hang out by the door and take a few pictures."

Max glanced over his shoulder. This wasn't exactly how he wanted to be viewed, as some kind of marketing tool. God, since his baseball career had taken off, he'd become a giant marketing machine— selling athletic shoes and luxury cars and expensive watches. He couldn't buy a pair of socks without having to think about the impact it would have on his endorsements. And every move he made in his personal life affected his ability to make money.

He hadn't really minded the notoriety that much... until the press showed it could also be nasty. Suddenly his day-to-day life had turned into fodder for media commentators. At first, he didn't care what was said about him because most of it had just been made up anyway. But when he'd learned his nieces and nephews were hearing about it at school, Max had decided to take a break from the spotlight.

A shoulder surgery he'd been putting off became the perfect chance to get out of the limelight, to give the media an opportunity to focus on someone else. And though he still had a few photographers waiting to catch him at a bad moment, his time in Chicago had given him a chance to really contemplate his future—after baseball.

Here, he could leave the temptations of New York and L.A. behind, the women, the partying, a nonstop glare of the camera flash. And the constant need to be selling something. "I'm just going to make a few calls," Max said. "I'll be in the office."

Max had purchased the bar in the DePaul neighborhood nearly a year ago, turning it over to his brother to renovate and run. Dave seemed to have a golden touch when it came to business. Whenever Max had money to invest, he turned it over to Dave, who managed to make them both rich.

At least Max didn't have to worry about how he was going to live after his baseball career ended. With seven years in the majors, he'd done pretty well for himself. Max smiled and shook hands as he walked back to the office, posing for a few photos along the way. When he finally closed the door behind him, he drew a deep breath and leaned back against it.

One day, he would be completely anonymous again. Max couldn't believe he'd ever been fearful of the moment when no one recognized him. Now, all he longed for was a normal life again. Since he'd been home, Max had quietly observed his three older siblings, all happily married with kids of their own, and wondered how they'd managed to find the key to the happiness.

They weren't famous, Max mused. Most of his old high school and college buddies envied him. He had everything they'd ever dreamed of having. Hell, he played a game for a living, traveling all over the country. He had more money than he'd ever need. And he was single. The women…well, the supply of beautiful women never seemed to wane.

Max reached up and rubbed his shoulder. There were a few drawbacks. He was in a constant fight with his aging body. And though he was a little more than a year shy of thirty, his body was already beginning to feel a lot older.

One thing always made the aches and pains disappear. Sex. And there were probably five or six girls sitting at the bar right now he could charm into his bed. But the prospect of losing himself in the plea-sures of a woman's body didn't seem all that exciting right now. Lately, his sexual conquests had always been followed by a juicy story in the tabloids. He couldn't completely trust anyone anymore, outside of his own family.

And since he'd returned, there hadn't been a single woman who'd caught his eye. Instead, he'd spent his time reviewing his business investments, rehabbing his shoulder and visiting with family. It's the injury, he thought to himself. The team doctor warned him he might experience some mild depression, that he'd need to focus more intently on his rehab and his re-turn in the second half of the season.

Max sat down at the desk and pulled out his cell phone, scrolling through the list of missed calls. Even though he was off the media radar, women were still interested. "Sophia," he murmured. An Italian model he met last month at a charity event. "Christina." A flight attendant who'd charmed him on his flight home from Tampa. "Helena." An actress he'd dated in New York during the off-season. Though a night in bed with a beautiful woman would certainly make him feel better, it just wasn't worth the hassle.

Max cursed softly and shut his phone, tossing it on the desk. What the hell was wrong with him? Making decisions about anything had become nearly impossible. He pushed to his feet and restlessly paced back and forth in the tiny office. "Do something," he muttered to himself. "Pick a lane and hit the Gas."

A soft knock sounded at the door and he looked up to see Dave peering inside. "Sorry to disturb, but Greg Wilbern, our liquor salesman is here and he'd really like to meet you. He brought his teenage son. This guy gives us great—"

Max held up his hand. "Say no more. I'll tell him his son looks like a future major leaguer."

"I wouldn't go that far. His son showed me how to reprogram our cash registers. I suspect he has a better chance working for Microsoft than in the major leagues."

Max followed Dave, closing the office door behind him. He glanced across the bar, scanning the crowd. Suddenly, his breath caught in his throat. She was sitting with a friend, sipping a drink, her warm blond hair softly falling around her face. She looked up and their gazes met and Max had an overwhelming feeling of déjà vu.

He stood, fixed in one spot, staring at her. They'd met before. Or maybe not. Yes, there had been a lot of women, but he remembered all of them—at least he thought he did. But, he'd never forgotten a woman he'd slept with.

"Are you coming?" Dave asked.

"Yeah, just give me a sec," Max murmured. "I'll be right over."

Had he ever touched her…or kissed her? His fingers twitched as he tried to recall the feel of her skin, her hair. What was the scent of her perfume? He had an uncanny memory for smells, but he couldn't re-call hers.

Max smiled and she returned it, tilting her head slightly. Whoever this woman was, he had to meet her. Maybe he did know her. "Think," he murmured. If he walked over and introduced himself and they'd already met, she'd be insulted. But if he acted as if he knew her, then she might be put off. "Best to be upfront." He took a step in her direction, finally pick-ing a lane and hitting the Gas.

"Max!"

Max blinked and looked at his brother motioning him toward the bar. He glanced back and the con-nection was broken. A strange sensation came over him. It was déjà vu. This had happened once before. When? Where had it been? He recalled the odd sense of loss he'd felt at the time.

Frustrated, Max approached the bar. Dave made the introductions, then handed Max a baseball from the stock they kept handy. "See that woman over there in the green dress? Send her a drink from me."

"Champagne?"

"No," Max said, as he scribbled his name the ball. "Never mind. That's too cheesy." He handed the boy the baseball, then shook the liquor salesman's hand. "I'll just go talk to her. Do I look all right? How's my breath? Shit, I shouldn't have had onions on that burger."

"What is wrong with you? Since when do you

worry about your appearance?" Dave looked over his shoulder. "That girl? She's not your type."

"What's my type?" Max asked.

"There's a ten sitting at the end of the bar. Fake hair, fake boobs, fake nails. She's your type."

"Shut up, Dave."

Max walked away from his brother and circled the bar slowly. Keeping his gaze fixed on her. Since the connection between them had been broken, she'd gone back to chatting with her girlfriend, a petite dark-haired woman with trendy glasses perched on her nose.

When he finally reached them, Max slipped into a spot next to her at the bar. But the patrons standing around her thought he'd come to socialize with them, wanting to shake his hand and pose for pictures. When the celebrity posturing was finally finished, he turned back to her.

"Hi," he said. Max waited for her to respond and began to think that she hadn't heard him, but then she slowly turned and faced him. She was even more beautiful up close. She had the greenest eyes he'd ever seen. And her shoulder-length hair, the color of honey, smelled like peaches.

"Hello," she said.

"Do I know you?"

She paused, then smiled quizzically. "I don't know. Do you?"

Max frowned. "I'm not sure. I can't believe I would have forgotten you if we'd met before." He held out his hand. "I'm Max. And forget what I just said. It sounded really lame."

"Angela," she said, resting her hand in his. She had beautiful fingers, long and slender, tipped with pretty red polish. No, Max thought. He'd never had those hands on his body. Though they might have met, they'd never been intimate. "And this is my friend, Celia. Ceci."

Max reached around to Ceci and shook her hand. "Hello, Ceci. It's nice to meet you." He turned back to Angela. "Can I buy you two a drink?"

Angela held up her margarita. "I have a drink. But thanks anyway."

"And I have to go," Ceci said. "I—I have to drive my mother—I mean, my brother to—shopping. I have to take my mother grocery shopping. She's completely out of...bananas." She forced a smile as she slid off her barstool. "Sorry, I forgot."

"Stay," Angela whispered, grabbing her hand. "How will you get home?"

"I'll grab a cab," Ceci said. "You just enjoy your drink." She picked up her purse, then gave Max a clever grin. "It was nice meeting you, Max. She likes her margaritas unblended, no salt. And she can't hold her liquor, so make the next one a virgin, all right?"

Max watched as Ceci hurried to the door. In any other instance, he would have been glad to have

Angela all to himself. But he felt strangely nervous. What the hell was that all about? Max Morgan never got nervous around women.

2

Angela took a quick sip of her drink. This was not part of the plan. Ceci wasn't supposed to leave the moment Max noticed her. They were supposed to stay together until Angela felt comfortable. They'd even worked out a series of signs and a plan to escape to the ladies' room to regroup if things got too complicated.

And they were already way too complicated. Her heart was slamming against the inside of her chest and she couldn't seem to catch her breath. And as she tried to calm herself, she felt light-headed and unable to think. Oh, God, she was having a…moment.

No, this wasn't supposed to happen! Angela knew exactly what Max Morgan was—a smooth operator. And yet she was allowing herself to be overwhelmed by his obvious magnetism. Get a grip, she scolded silently. You're a grown woman with a job to do. This is no time for silly fantasies.

But if she couldn't even think of something clever

to say, how would she keep him interested long enough to get all her questions answered? What if he decided to move on to someone else after just a few short minutes? She'd be left sitting alone at the bar feeling like a fool, humiliated in public.

But then, maybe that would be for the best. If he dumped her for someone prettier, it would only prove her point—Max Morgan was a class-A jerk.

"So," Max said. "Do you come here often?"

Angela swallowed hard. How many times had she heard that line? He was supposed to be an expert at seduction and that was the best he could come up with? "You really need to work on your pick-up lines."

The words were out of her mouth before she had a chance to think. Oh, hell, she'd just insulted him. And given him an excuse to move on to the redhead at the end of the bar.

At first, he seemed a bit taken aback by her comment. But then Max laughed and slid onto the stool vacated by Ceci. He thought she was teasing him. She could use that to her advantage. Keep him off balance. He was obviously used to having women agree with everything he said. She'd do the opposite. Reverse psychology.

"I do," Max said. "And that was really bad. Maybe I should move right on to astrological signs. Wait, here's a good one. I think I need to call heaven because they're missing one of their angels. How does that work for you?"

Angela had to admit, he'd gone from cheesy to charming in a heartbeat. Max had a way of looking at her with those dark and dangerous eyes that made her feel as though she was the most captivating female on the planet. But that was all part of the package that was Max Morgan, Sexy Devil. He could tempt even the most steadfast of women. "Sweet and not at all suggestive. A good effort. I'd give it a seven out of ten."

"Oh, you want suggestive? You must be the reason for global warming because you're hot."

"No," Angela said, shaking her head. "Not good to reference the looks. It makes you appear shallow and desperate. That one deserves a two."

"I lost my number, can I have yours?"

"Clever. Not as trite as the previous attempt."

"If I followed you home, would you keep me?"

Angela groaned. All right, he was impossibly charming. But she certainly wasn't going to let that affect her in the least. "Do you have a database of these? Or is your memory really that good?"

He leaned closer. "I have more. Maybe if you'd tell me what would work, I could choose more wisely."

He was obviously interested. But how far was he planning to take this, she wondered. Was he simply having a little fun or was he looking for something more. Angela gathered her nerve. "Sorry. Pick-up lines don't work with me," she said.

"What's the worst you've ever heard?" he asked.

"If I had a garden, I'd put your tulips and my tulips together? Just how is that supposed to work?"

Max leaned forward and brushed his lips across hers, lingering there for a brief moment before stepping back. "I think it worked pretty well."

Stunned, Angela stared at him. Yes, it was an innocent kiss, so quick it barely warranted mention. But she hadn't had a chance to prepare herself. Max Morgan, the man of her teenage dreams, had just kissed her! That simple touch had a startling effect on her body. Her pulse began racing and a warm flush crept up her cheeks. She opened her mouth, then quickly snapped it shut. Any attempt to put together a clever comeback would result in a string of incoherent babble.

His expression shifted suddenly and she thought she saw a flash of regret cross his deeply tanned face. "Hey, I'm sorry," he said. "I didn't mean anything by that. Really." He grabbed her hand. "Maybe we could start over? I'm Max Morgan. And the reason I came over here was to tell you that you look incredible in that dress. The color is…amazing."

Angela cleared her throat, trying to regain her composure. Rewind. Begin again. Gather your composure and act as if the kiss meant nothing. It didn't mean anything at all! "That was a pretty good line. Honesty. I like that."

"I was an Eagle Scout. We're big on honesty."

"I know," she said. She knew every arcane detail about Max. "I mean, Eagle Scouts are supposed to be trustworthy, right? You should have probably led with that instead of the angel line."

He held out his hand. "Hello, I'm Max Morgan, former Eagle Scout."

"Angela Weatherby," she replied. "Former ..." What could she say. Wallflower? Introvert? Stalker? "President of the Latin Club."

"Really?" he asked. "So, you're smart and beautiful."

"And you're cheeky and charming," Angela replied.

Max pushed away from the bar. "Would you like to get out of here? It's a nice night. Why don't we take a walk?"

She felt a tremor run through her. This was the moment of truth. She could turn and run or she could hang in there and get her interview. Angela pointed to her shoes. "I'm not going far in these heels."

"I know the perfect place, then," he said.

She wasn't sure she'd be able to handle Max on her own, without the distractions of the bar to fill the silences. But this was her chance, to figure out this guy who'd had such a hold on her. And to rationalize her crazy reaction to him. "Sure," she said. "That sounds nice." In truth, it sounded impossibly romantic.

"All right, here's the plan. Where is your car parked?"

"In the ramp just down the block."

"Why don't you leave through the front door and

start walking toward the ramp. I'll go out the back and meet you outside. That way, nobody will see us leaving together."

Angela frowned. "That was not a good line," she said. "In fact, it was kind of insulting."

"No!" he cried, taking her hand again. "No, no. That's not what I meant. It's just that if we leave together, there will be all kinds of speculation, maybe even some mention of it in the papers. I don't want you to get pulled into that." He paused. "You know who I am, don't you?"

Angela decided not to lie. What would be the point? She just stared at him silently and shrugged. "You're Max Morgan," she replied. "You play baseball."

He grabbed her hand. "Come on, we'll both go out the back." He laced his fingers between hers and pulled her along behind him, through the crowd to the kitchen and then out the rear door to the alley. "We'll take my car." He pointed to a black BMW sedan with tinted windows, parked against the building.

Max opened the passenger side door for her and helped her inside, then hopped in behind the wheel. Angela wasn't sure what to say to him. She'd expected they might chat at the bar. She'd been prepared to ask him a few questions, to get a sense of the man he was. She'd even predicted it would take approximately thirty minutes for her to realize, once and for all, that he was not the man of her post-adolescent dreams.

The night was definitely not going as planned. "Nice car," she murmured.

He laughed as he reached for the ignition. "Now, I'm going to have to start calling you out on the cheesy lines."

"Sorry," Angela said, relaxing a bit. "I'm not the best flirt. And I'm sure that's what you're used to."

Max turned to her. "Maybe I don't like what I'm used to," he said. "Maybe I don't want you to flirt with me." He shook his head. "Sometimes I just wish people could forget all that celebrity stuff and be normal."

"Well, if you're looking for normal, then I'm definitely it," Angela said. "Nothing very special here."

"You were president of the Latin Club," he said, grinning. "I think that's kind of special."

"You're very strange," Angela said. As he pulled out of the parking spot, she took the opportunity to observe him, his profile outlined by the light from the street lamps.

He was even more beautiful than she remembered, his features so perfectly. His hair was darker and his body more mature, but there was still a bit of the handsome boy left inside him—especially in the smile and in the teasing tone of his voice.

"Tell me something completely random about yourself. Let's start there."

Angela knew she'd have to come up with something intriguing and humorous. Something to show him that an evening with her could be fun. "I can list all the states in the Union."

"Impressive," Max said.

"In alphabetical order, in reverse alpha order, in order of entrance into the union, and in order of geographical size. Plus I know all of the capitals by heart." She drew a deep breath. "What can I say, I was a geek and my parents thought it was an interesting party trick."

"You are a very interesting woman, Angela." He turned on some music, flipping through the CDs in his player until he found something soothing.

She was going to make a complete mess of things. In another hour, he'd be dropping her off at the parking ramp and heading back to the bar, looking for someone more intriguing. It was time to start asking questions. "So you're famous," she ventured. "What's that like?"

"It's about what you'd expect," he said with a shrug. "Sometimes bad, sometimes good."

"Tell me the bad," Angela said.

"I hate the press. I hate that they can make up stories about my life without any thought of how it affects the people I love. I hate that people wonder who I date or where I eat dinner or where I sleep at night. I hate that I don't have much of a life outside of baseball."

"Tell me the good," she said.

"If I wasn't famous, you might not have given

me a second look at the bar," he said. "I'm glad you did."

"Oh, you think I'm impressed by your fame?" Angela asked. "I've spent time with much more famous people than you—Churchill, Gandhi, Hemingway. You don't impress me."

"Obviously not," Max said with a devilish grin. "Since you seem intent on poking holes in my ego." He opened all the windows in the BMW, letting the warm summer wind blow through the car. "I love Chicago in the summer. The smell, the sounds. I never get to enjoy my summers anymore. It's always about work, the next game, the next at bat. This is the first summer in my memory that I haven't played baseball."

"Isn't it fun?" she asked, anxious to keep him talking about himself.

"It's a job. It can be fun. It certainly looks like fun. But it's not...normal. I'd like to lead a normal life."

"Normal is boring," Angela said. "Take it from me."

"Normal might be nice for a change." He glanced over at her. "What would you be doing on a normal Tuesday night?"

"Laundry," she said.

"You made the right decision," he teased. "I'm much more interesting than laundry."

The conversation was going well. Maybe it was time to get a bit more personal. "Can I ask you a question?" Angela began.

"Anything," he said.

"Why did you choose me? That bar was full of women more beautiful. More interested in a guy like you. Why me?"

"I don't know," Max said. "I just got this feeling. When I saw you and our eyes met, there was this… moment."

Angela's breath froze in her throat. Oh, God. He'd had a moment, too? What did that mean? No, there was no need to get excited. Maybe a guy like him had multiple moments. Maybe it didn't mean anything at all. Of course, they'd been attracted to each other. But a "moment" was more than just sexual attraction, wasn't it?

They chatted about a variety of subjects for the rest of the ride—the latest festivals on the lakefront, the best ethnic restaurants in town, the traffic, the weather. But Angela couldn't get her mind off the "moment."

The conversation turned to his injury and his rehab efforts, but she found herself transfixed by a careful study of his mouth. He asked her about her work and she told him she was in communications, before changing the subject to the music he liked.

By the time they reached the lake, the conversation had become surprisingly relaxed, at least to the casual observer. But Angela was in the midst of an internal crisis. She found herself completely charmed by Max Morgan. He was sweet and funny and smart. And when he smiled at her, she felt as if she might just melt into a big puddle of goo on his leather seat.

No, Angela thought to herself. Max Morgan was supposed to be the enemy. And all this charm was expected from a smooth operator. Of course, he would try to weaken her defenses, to turn himself into the perfect guy. He knew exactly how to read the signs. And if she weren't careful, she'd fall for it, hook, line and sinker.

Max found a place to park, then helped her out of the car. It was dark on the beach, but the city was alive with light behind them. He held onto her arm as she kicked off her shoes and stepped into the sand. Then he laced his fingers through hers and they walked toward the water.

"I never come to the beach," she said. "I just drive by." She closed her eyes and drew a deep breath. "It doesn't smell like the city."

"I have a place on the water in Florida," he said. "And a place on a small lake in Wisconsin. And my apartment here in Chicago overlooks the lake. I'm a water guy, I guess. Where do you live?"

"I have a flat in Wicker Park." This guy was seriously out of her league, Angela thought to herself. He had at least three homes, maybe even more. She lived in a tiny, one-bedroom flat with leaky pipes and a noisy radiator.

When they reached the water's edge, Max slipped out of his shoes and socks and rolled up his pant legs, then waded in. "Cold," he said, wincing. "I can't believe I used to swim in this."

"It's always cold," Angela said, backing away from his invitation to join him. He ran out and grabbed her, pulling her along until her toes touched the water too.

"No!" she cried, trying to twist out of his grasp. But he pulled her closer until she was caught in his embrace. He stared down into her eyes, then bent closer and kissed her.

Angela tried to remain calm, hoping to remember every little detail of the kiss. It was sweet and simple and filled with a delicious anticipation. She parted her lips and he took the invitation to tease at her tongue. He'd obviously had a lot of experience kissing women and it had paid off. When he finally drew away, she felt as if her legs were about to buckle beneath her.

"I've been thinking about doing that ever since we left the bar," he murmured, smoothing his hand through her hair. His gaze scanned her features and he smiled. "I don't know what it is. I feel like we know each other. Is that strange?"

"Yes," Angela said. The one word was all she could manage for the moment. Oh, it was wonderful kissing him. And though she'd tried to maintain her defenses, it was all it took to make her realize that she was totally and utterly at his mercy.

He pulled her back into his arms and kissed her

again, this time more playfully. "So, what are we going to do for our next date?"

"What?"

"Where are we going to go? You probably have to work tomorrow, but I'm free tomorrow night. We can go to dinner or take in a concert. I haven't been to the aquarium for years."

Angela wasn't sure what to say. This was so unexpected. Although, maybe he'd do the same thing all the other smooth operators did—promise to call her tomorrow to firm up their plans and then never call. "I—I don't know. I'd have to check my—"

He placed a finger over her lips. "No. We're going to plan it now. I'll pick you up at six."

Angela took a deep breath. She wasn't sure she wanted to believe what he was saying. She'd have more than just this night to get to know Max. All the questions spinning around in her head didn't have to be asked tonight. Tonight, she could just enjoy herself. "Six," she said in a shaky voice. "Sounds good."

THEY SAT ON THE SAND for two hours, talking, joking, laughing. Max couldn't remember the last time he'd been so completely fascinated by a woman. What was it about Angela that he found so sexy? Had he passed her on the street or seen her at a party, he might have considered her ordinary.

But for the first time, he found himself looking a bit deeper. She was a study in contrasts. One moment she was confident and outspoken and the next, shy and nervous. She didn't play games, but she did enjoy poking at his ego every so often. And though she wasn't the kind of woman he usually found himself attracted to, he was beginning to think she was the most beautiful woman he'd ever met.

"This is going to be a great summer," Max said.

"Will you have the entire summer off?" Angie asked.

"If rehab goes well, I should be on my way back to the club by September. Maybe August. But I'm thinking I need time, not just to heal physically, but to figure out a few things."

"Like what?" Angie asked, turning to face him.

He grabbed her legs and pulled them over his, drawing her close to kiss her. The impulse to seduce her was overwhelming. He wanted to explore her body, to learn what made her shudder with desire. There was something between them that he'd never experienced before. Yet, he didn't want her to be just another notch on his bedpost.

"Like life," he said. "I've been living in an alternate reality. I see my brothers and sisters and their families and they're happy. Really happy, not just artificially happy."

"How can you be artificially happy?" she asked.

"You know. When you buy a new car and you think you're happy, and maybe you are for a day or so. But then you realize it's just a car."

Angela leaned against him, the warmth from her

body seeping into his. "So what makes you really happy?"

"Kissing you does it for me," he said.

"Then do it," she said.

This time, he put aside the gentle, sweet kisses they'd shared. Max wanted her to know exactly how he felt about her. His lips found hers and he slowly lowered her into the sand, stretching out beside her.

His hand smoothed over her arms and then lower, to her hip. As she drew her leg up, her skirt fell away and he touched the silky length of her calf. It was so easy to get lost in the feel and taste of her. At first, he didn't notice the wind picking up, swirling the sand around him.

And then, a moment later, the clouds opened and it began to rain. Max rolled to his side and looked up at the sky. Nature had decided to mess with his perfect date. But to his surprise, Angela didn't seem to care. Instead, she sat up, turned her face to the sky and laughed.

The downpour had already drenched her hair and her dress, and droplet clung to her lashes. She opened her mouth to catch the rain with her tongue and Max could only watch her. Any other woman would be racing for cover, hoping to preserve her carefully tended appearance. But that obviously hadn't occurred to Angela.

Thunder rumbled in the distance and when lightning flashed, Max leapt to his feet and grabbed her hand. "Come on. Let's get out of here before we get zapped."

As they ran to the car, pedestrians were rushing for cover. He unlocked the door and pulled it open, then helped her inside. When he finally slipped in behind the wheel, she was raking her fingers through her dripping hair. "I'm getting your car all wet," she said. "And my dress is covered with sand."

"Don't worry." He pulled out into traffic and headed north on Lakeshore Drive. "My condo is just on the other side of the zoo," he said. "We'll stop there, get dried off and then decide what we want to do with the rest of the night." He glanced over at the clock in the dashboard and was surprised to see that it was past midnight. "Or, I could drop you back at your car," he added. "You probably have to be up early for work tomorrow."

"I really wouldn't mind getting dry," she said.

Good, Max thought to himself. He didn't want the night to end, either. Not yet. Not until he was absolutely sure she wanted him as much as he wanted her.

Minutes later, he pulled into the underground garage of his Lincoln Park high rise. As they rode the elevator up, he pressed her back against the wall and kissed her again, his fingers tangling in her damp hair. "This has been the most amazing night," he whispered.

She stared up at him, a strange look in her eyes. Didn't she believe him? Hell, that was all he needed.

The first time he found a woman he was truly interested in and she thought he was playing her. So how could he prove he wasn't, Max wondered. He could forget about luring her into his bed. That would be a good start.

"Your lips taste like rain," he murmured. When the elevator doors opened, he took her hand and walked with her to the door of his apartment. He pushed the key into the lock, then stepped aside to let her enter. The apartment was dark, rain glittering on the wide wall of windows overlooking the lake.

He wanted to draw her into his arms again, now that they were completely alone, and find out just how deep their attraction for each other went. Instead, he flipped on the lights. "The bathroom is just down that hall," Max said. "There are towels in the cabinet and I'll find you some dry clothes."

He watched as she walked away from him, her wet dress clinging to her slender body. Somehow, he knew the night wasn't over. It was just beginning.

Max hurried to his bedroom and rummaged through his clothes for something to give her. He found a team sweatshirt and some warm-up pants, then grabbed a pair of socks from the clean laundry.

When he knocked softly on the bathroom door, Angie opened it a crack and he held the clothes out. "It's the best I can do," he said. "They're warm and they're dry."

"Is it all right if I take a quick shower?" she asked. "I'm covered with sand."

"No problem," he said. "I'm just going to make us something to eat. Are you hungry?"

"Yeah," she said with a winsome smile. "That would be great." She took the clothes and shut the door. He glanced at his watch. He had about ten minutes tops to shower, get dressed and cook something. Max headed to the galley kitchen and to his relief, found a container of gourmet mac and cheese he'd bought at Whole Foods. He popped it into the oven and headed for the guest bathroom.

As he stepped beneath the hot water, his mind wandered down the hall, to the woman who was showering in his bathroom. With any other woman, he wouldn't have thought twice about joining her there. And with any other woman, he knew he'd have been welcome. But he didn't want to move too fast with Angela. He was having trouble reading her signals and a single mistake might win it all.

Max glanced down and groaned. Just the thought of the two of them naked together brought a physical reaction. He turned up the cold water and stood beneath it until the spray stung his skin. Then he stepped out, grabbed a towel and wrapped it around his waist.

He hurried back through the living room, dripping water on the hardwood floors. But he stopped suddenly when he saw Angela standing at the windows, peering down at the street. She turned and her eyes went wide when she noticed he was dressed only in a damp towel.

To his relief, the cold water had done the trick and there wasn't an embarrassing bulge in the front of that damp towel. "Sorry," Max muttered, clutching at the cotton where it was tucked around his waist. "I thought you'd take a little longer in the shower."

"I didn't want to take advantage," she said. "It's a nice shower. Big...enough for two."

"I—I'm just going to go get dressed. I'll be right back."

When he returned from the bedroom, wearing basketball shorts and a T-shirt, Angela was still standing at the window. He stepped up behind her, then slipped his arms around her waist. "What do you see out there?"

"It's a beautiful view. It's so quiet up here."

Max rested his chin on her shoulder. "The minute I saw this place, I knew I had to have it. And there was no way I'd stay at my parents' place. My mother would drive me crazy and my father would expect me to help him with all of his household repair projects. I needed a place of my own here in Chicago."

"So you dropped a few million on a condo? Why not rent?"

"It seemed like a good investment," Max said. "And now that I've been here for a while, I like it. It feels like home." He turned her around to face him. "What can I get you to drink? I have wine. And beer. Energy drinks and mineral water."

"A glass of wine would be nice," Angela said. "Red, if you have it."

As Max walked to the kitchen, he smiled to himself. This was going well. She could have asked for a ride home. But instead, she'd stay at least long enough to finish a glass of wine and eat some mac and cheese. He found a bottle, struggled with the cork, then filled a wineglass nearly to the brim.

It would take her longer to drink a big glass of wine, giving him more time. But at the last minute he dumped half of it in the sink. She might think he was trying to get her drunk. He didn't want to confirm all the worst things the press had to say about him.

"Take it slow," he reminded himself. "And don't make an ass of yourself."

Angela pressed her hand to her chest. Ever since he'd walked into the room, dressed in a only a towel, she hadn't been able to breathe. It had been a long time since she'd been in the presence of a naked man—or a nearly naked one. Almost a year. And she'd never been near a man with a body like Max's. The fact that it was Max, the man of her teenage fantasies, made the entire incident surreal.

After he'd walked away, she'd thought about following him, about tugging the towel off the lower part of his body and exploring everything underneath. If she were only bolder, she could do something like that.

But Angela knew the dangers of allowing herself

to surrender to a guy like Max. Though she wanted to believe that he genuinely liked her, she couldn't help but wonder if this stop at his apartment was all part of a grand plan to seduce her. There was no ignoring the profiles on her Web site. Max did have an amazing capacity to separate a woman from her panties.

If he wasn't interested in sex, then why had he brought her here? Angela suspected it had nothing to do with getting warm and dry. He'd probably waltzed through in a towel on purpose, just to tempt her. And she was tempted. It would be so easy to fall into his trap, to make the first move so he couldn't be blamed for the seduction.

Angela had indulged in a few one-night stands over the years, only to regret her behavior the next day. But would she regret sleeping with Max? She'd finally have a chance to make her teenage fantasies come true. How many women would pass up a chance like that? If he were great, then she'd have a memory to keep for the rest of her life. And if he wasn't, maybe she could finally consign her fantasies to the past.

If he offered, she'd accept, Angela decided. But what if he didn't offer? What would that mean? Was she not woman enough to satisfy him? Though she hadn't had the number of experiences that he'd had, Angela knew how to pleasure a man. She was good in bed. Not porn-star good, but she could get a little kinky when called for.

"Here. Red wine. Dinner should be ready in about ten minutes."

Angela jumped at the sound of his voice. She turned and took the glass from his hand. "What are you cooking? It smells good."

"Mac and cheese. I buy it in bulk from Whole Foods."

"I love their mac and cheese," she said. "And I am a little hungry. I haven't stayed up this late for a long time."

"You don't go out much?"

Angela shook her head. "No. I don't really like the bar scene."

"What were you doing out tonight?"

"It was just a whim," she lied. "Ceci convinced me to go. What about you? Do you do this often?"

"Drink wine?"

"Bring a girl home?" She might as well get a few more of her questions answered. "You're very difficult to resist. Very…charming."

"I'm having a nice time just talking to you, Angela. I'm not looking for anything else."

"You aren't?"

"No. I mean, I think it's a little early to—not that I wouldn't want to. You're beautiful. Any man would want to…you know. But I think we should just let things happen…."

Angela set her wineglass down on the windowsill. So how did he feel? Was he having second thoughts about seducing her? Didn't he think she could handle it? Well, she was just as capable of enjoying it as any other woman. "Why don't you kiss me again and we'll see what happens?"

She'd be crazy not to take the chance when she had it, right? Forget the book, forget all the questions she wanted to ask. Her curiosity had completely overwhelmed her common sense and she wanted to enjoy what so many other women had.

It didn't take him more than a heartbeat to change his mind. His fingers slipped through her hair and he pulled her mouth to his, steering her toward the sofa. This time, his kiss left no doubt in her mind as to where they were headed. He couldn't seem to get enough of her lips and her tongue. Max was like a man, parched with thirst and desperately searching for a cool taste of water.

They tumbled onto the leather cushions and he pulled her down on top of him, his hands roaming freely over her body. There wasn't much between them. Angela had left her underwear to dry in the bathroom and Max hadn't bothered with his, either.

When he slipped his hand beneath the hem of the sweatshirt and skimmed it up her back, she moaned. It was the most delicious sensation in the world. Every nerve seemed to tingle as his touch drifted from one spot to the next.

In the past, Angela had always kept a small part of herself detached from the man sharing her bed, afraid to commit herself completely, afraid that she might be making a mistake. But with Max, she wanted to surrender, wanted to offer him every pleasure that he might find her in body. It was just one night, that's all. Why not enjoy it completely?

She was breathless and giddy. Though Angela knew the risks, her body was on fire, the desire so hot that the only way to survive was to tear off all her clothes. Straddling his hips, she sat up and tugged the sweatshirt over her head. Her hair tumbled around her face as she tossed the sweatshirt aside. Angela watched as he slowly reached out to cup her breast in his palm. She closed her eyes and tipped her head back, losing touch with reality.

Was this a dream? Would she wake up suddenly, alone in her bed, and realize that once again, her fantasies of him were just an illusion? No, Angela thought. She felt her skin tingle where he touched and she heard the pulse pounding through her veins. She smelled the scent of his cologne and heard the sound of his breathing.

If this wasn't real, it was the most vivid dream she'd ever experienced. Angela stared into his eyes, daring the image to fade before her. But instead, he drew her down again, into another kiss, this one, more powerful than the last.

"What are we doing?" he whispered

"Touching," she said. "Kissing."

He groaned softly as she shifted above him, his hard shaft pressed against the spot between her legs. It wouldn't take much to rid themselves of the rest of their clothes. Angela knew so much about him, yet all of it was purely superficial. She wanted to see him naked, to touch him intimately and to have those images burned into her memory. "Take your shirt off," she whispered.

Max pushed up on his elbows and she pulled his shirt over his head, then dropped it on the floor. Angela ran her palms over his torso, from his belly to his chest, the muscle rippling beneath her fingers.

He was absolute perfection, his skin smooth and warm and burnished brown by the sun. Angela smiled, wondering at how this fantasy had suddenly become reality. Every time she thought it might end, it just got better and better. Perhaps this was the way it was meant to happen between them. This was the time when they'd both be at their best, the time when they could both walk away with out any regrets.

She ran her hands along his arms, then laced her fingers between his, drawing his arms up above his head. Nuzzling her face into the curve of his neck, she leaned closer, her breasts rubbing against his chest.

Max groaned, then grabbed her around the waist. Before she knew what was happening, he was standing beside the sofa, her legs wrapped around his hips. He carried her down the hall, toward his bedroom. Angela knew if she had any doubts, now was the time to call an end to this. But she wanted to go the rest of the way, to share the ultimate intimacy with him.

He stopped halfway down the hall and gently pushed her into the wall, his mouth coming down on hers for a deep, demanding kiss. She arched against him until they were nearly joined, their clothes providing the last barrier between anticipation and release.

Max groaned again, then suddenly went still. Angela waited, wondering what had happened. Then with a sinking feeling, she knew what it was. The excitement had been too much for him. "It's all right," she whispered, toying with a lock of his damp hair. "We can just wait a bit."

He drew back and a gasp slipped from his throat. "What?"

"I understand. It happens. Things were pretty intense there."

"You think I …" His voice trailed off and then he laughed. "No, I'm fine. Everything is still fully… functional."

"Then why did you stop?"

"Because I'm really not sure we should be doing this, Angela. In fact, I'm positive we shouldn't be doing this. Not yet. Not that I don't really, really want to do this. Believe me, I do. But, I think if we both take a step back and—"

Angela quickly unwound her legs from his waist and dropped to her feet. As her body slid against his, she noticed that the bulge in his shorts wasn't subsiding. Oh, God. She'd just assumed he'd— "Right," she said, nodding frantically. "You're absolutely right. I mean, we've just met. And I understand you probably have women coming on to you all the time. It must be so—"

"No!" Max said, reaching out to touch her face. "It's not that. Believe me." He drew a deep breath, then let it out slowly. "I'm just going to get the rest of our clothes. Then we can—talk. We'll talk. And eat."

As he strode toward the living room, Angela braced herself against the wall, holding her arms over her breasts. What was going on? Didn't he want her? Wasn't she attractive enough for him to take to bed? This was not the behavior of a smooth operator.

First Alex Stamos, then Charlie Templeton and now, Max Morgan. Why couldn't these men behave the way they were supposed to? What was happening to the world as she knew it? Every assumption she'd made about these seducers was being shattered. And now, Max Morgan was acting all upright and honorable.

When he returned, Max was wearing his T-shirt again. He helped her into the sweatshirt, then took her hand and led her back to the sofa. He sat down next to her, then grabbed her hands and kissed the tips of her fingers.

"I had a really nice time tonight," he said. "I want to see you again. And I don't want to mess anything up by sleeping together just a few hours after we met."

"Is that really why you stopped," Angela asked.

"Or is that just the story you think I'll buy until you can get me out of your apartment?"

"I don't know how much you know about me, or my rather formidable reputation with the ladies. But most of it is greatly exaggerated by the press." He paused. "Well, some of it is true, but a lot isn't."

"So, when you bring a woman home, you usually sleep with her?"

He drew in a sharp breath, then nodded. "Usually."

"Why not me?" Angela asked, desperate to know the answer.

"Because you're someone I'd like to know better. That is, if you want to get to know me."

She searched his eyes for the truth in his words, but Angela didn't know him well enough to guess at what was really beneath his reluctance. No man, not even the most well-intentioned red-blooded male, would turn down the chance at sex. There had to be something more to this.

She forced a smile, then quickly stood. "I—I have to get up early for work tomorrow. I should really get home."

"You're not hungry?"

"No."

Max cupped her face with his hand, his forehead meeting hers. Then he kissed her, the contact soft and fleeting. "All right. I'll take you back to your car."

"No," Angela said. "I can get a cab."

"I'll take you," Max insisted, his tone firm, yet betraying a hint of irritation.

"I'll just get my things." She stepped around him and walked back to the bathroom. When she got inside, she closed the door behind her. Angela caught sight of herself in the wide mirror that hung on the wall above the sinks. She leaned closer to examine her face.

She was still flushed, her cheeks pink and her lips red and puffy. Her hair, though mussed, didn't look that bad. Objectively, she should have been pretty enough to tempt Max into sex.

Angela fought back a wave of anger. She knew exactly what kind of man Max Morgan was and she'd allowed herself to get carried away by his charm. It was all there in black-and-white on her Web site. What made her think that he'd be any different with her?

This was all Ceci's fault, all of her talk about "moments" and "hope springing eternal." Max was exactly what she knew him to be—a smooth operator. Of course, he wouldn't want a woman like her. He never noticed the girl she'd been, so why would he even consider the woman she'd become?

She wouldn't get her fantasy night with Max Morgan after all. Tomorrow, she'd wait for his call and it wouldn't come. And in a few weeks, she'd find out he was dating another woman—a model or an actress, someone more befitting his status in the celebrity world.

He was everything she knew him to be—a rogue, a cad, a seducer and the shallowest man she'd ever met. But she would get one thing she wanted from this night—an end to all of her silly fantasies. She'd never have to think of him again and wonder what may have been. Though they might have shared a moment, it was *the* moment.

Angela pulled off his clothes and slipped into her own underwear and dress. She winced at the cold, damp fabric against her skin, the sand still caught in the seams and folds. The sooner this night was over, the better.

3

MAX GLANCED OVER AT Angela, her profile outlined by the lights from the street. They'd made a quick exit from his place and an uneasy silence had enveloped them. He wasn't quite sure how to read her expression. At first glance, she seemed unbothered by what had happened between them. But experience had taught him that how a woman acted and how she really felt could be two completely different things.

The night had been so promising, but it was ending on a sour note. Maybe he should have taken her to bed. She seemed almost insulted that he hadn't. But for the first time in his life, Max had looked past his urges and put aside his need for release. He wanted a good life after baseball and a woman to share it with. Seducing every woman who caught his eye wasn't getting him there. So maybe it was time to try a different approach.

It was his mistake. He shouldn't have started what he didn't want to finish. They should have kept their clothes on, sipped their wine and eaten a little mac and cheese. He would have driven her back, they would have kissed good-night and he could have looked forward to a second date. Now, he wasn't even sure he ought to try to kiss her again.

Max glanced over to see Angela rub her bare arms and he reached for the air conditioner. "Are you cold?" he asked.

"No," she said.

"You're rubbing your arms."

She forced a smile. "I'm fine."

With a muttered curse, he shut off the air conditioner and rolled down the windows, letting the warm night breeze flow through the car. Was this what he deserved for trying to be a gentleman? That's what women were supposed to want, right? A guy who wasn't focused on getting into their pants? It wasn't just supposed to be about sex. There was trust and friendship, too.

He'd wanted to explain his reasoning to her, but Max suspected he'd only make things worse. So, for now, he'd just stay quiet, get her number before he dropped her off, and they would start fresh on their next date.

As they neared the parking ramp, he began to worry that she might not give him her number at all. He pulled into the ramp and grabbed the ticket, then turned to her. "Where are you parked?" he asked.

"Level 3B," she said. "It's a blue Volkswagen Jetta."

Max carefully steered up the spiral ramp and exited on the third level, then squinted in the low light, looking for her car.

"It's right there," she said, pointing to the left.

Max took an empty spot nearby, then turned off the BMW. She made to get out of the car, but he reached out and took her arm. "Hang on." He grabbed his cell phone from the center console. "I don't have your number."

"Why do you need my number?" she asked.

She was angry. Much angrier than he'd ever suspected. "Because we have a date tomorrow and I want to call you and work out the details."

"We made those plans before..." Her voice trailed off and she waited for him to reply.

He sent her an inquiring look. "Before what? Before I decided we shouldn't sleep together?" He shook his head. "It isn't always about sex, no matter what you might have read in the press."

With an impatient sigh, she rattled off a series of numbers. He punched them into his cell phone, then smiled in relief. "All right. I'll call you. Tomorrow."

She made a move for the door again, but Max wasn't about to let her get away without one last kiss. He smoothed his hand along the length of her arm, then tangled his fingers in her hair. Angela turned toward him. He leaned forward and dropped a simple kiss on her lips. "I'll see you tomorrow."

"Tomorrow," she murmured. With that, she made

her escape. Max turned on the BMW and waited until she was safely inside her car, before pulling out behind her. He followed her down to street level. She turned left and he thought about following her home. But at the last minute, he decided to go back to the bar and help his brother close. Right now, he needed some advice from a guy who had actually managed to find a woman to love.

When he pulled into his parking spot behind the bar, he reached for his phone. On a whim, he decided to call her, just to see if he could smooth things over a bit more. He dialed the number and waited. It rang twice.

"Thai Express," the voice on the other end of the line said. "Pick-up or delivery?"

"Shit," he muttered.

"May I help you?"

"Sorry," Max said. "Wrong number." He checked the call against her number. He'd dialed the digits she'd given him. Either he'd messed up entering it on his phone or she'd deliberately given him a bad number.

He got out of the car and walked through the back door of the bar. The kitchen had closed an hour before and a few members of the staff were still cleaning up. When he entered the bar, there was still a crowd, but it wasn't nearly as busy as it had been earlier. He noticed Caroline, one of their best bartenders, behind the bar. "Is Dave still here?"

"In the office," she said. "Can you tell him we're

running low on rimming salt. I used the last container to make the rim mix for the Bloody Marys."

"No problem," Max said. A few people caught him on the way to the office but he still managed to get through the crowd pretty quickly. When he shut the door behind him, he found Dave on the computer, clicking through the liquor inventory.

"Caroline says you need more rimming salt. She used the last of it for the Bloody Mary stuff. Why don't you just order Bloody Mary salt?"

"Because we mix our own," Dave murmured. "We're known for our Bloody Marys. We sell a ton of them on Bloody Sundays. Ten bucks a pop."

"For tomato juice and vodka?" Max asked.

"Not just that. It's the garbage we add. A special salt on the rim, a shot of stuff that packs a punch, and a skewer that includes all kinds of pickled veggies. You should try one."

"I could use one right now," Max said, flopping down in a nearby chair.

Dave grabbed the phone and buzzed the bar. "Carrie, can you bring Max one of our Bloodies. Make it a good one." He hung up the phone, then turned to face his brother. "What are you doing back here?"

"I thought I'd come back and help you close."

His brother's eyebrow shot up and he gave Max a dubious look. "You left with a woman. I figured you'd be busy for the rest of the evening."

"I don't sleep with every woman I meet," Max said.

"Yes, you do. All the magazines say you do."

"Screw the magazines," Max muttered. "They said I was Madonna's new boytoy. I've never even met the woman. Don't believe everything you read."

"It didn't work out with the girl?" Dave asked.

"No, the girl was great. We made a date for tomorrow night—I guess that would be tonight."

"So, you two didn't …"

"No. This girl is…different. I don't know what it is. She's really sweet and kind of shy. But she sees right through me. I mean, she doesn't fall for my bullshit. And I feel like I know her." He paused. "Do you believe in reincarnation?"

"You think you shared a past life?"

"No. But it's like that." He sighed. "The only problem is, I don't have her phone number. I must have entered it wrong in my phone. I tried calling and I got a Thai restaurant."

"She gave you a bad number," Dave said, chuckling. "Oh, isn't that sweet. You finally meet a girl worth dating and she doesn't want you. Max Morgan has lost his mojo."

"It was probably just an innocent mistake."

"You think?" Dave asked.

"I'll just look her up in the book."

"What's her name?" Dave asked, turning back to the computer. "I'll look her up online."

"Angela Weatherly. Or maybe it's Weatherby." He groaned. "Shit. It's Weather-something." As Dave was searching the online phone book, Caroline came in with a huge glass, filled with Dave's version of a Bloody Mary. "Jeez, this thing is a meal," Max muttered.

"There isn't an A. Weatherby listed. There is an A. Weatherly listed."

"That must be it," Max said. "What's the address?"

"Looks like Lakeview," he said.

"She said she lives in Wicker Park," Max said. "You think I should try that one?"

"At two in the morning? No." Dave paused. "Give me her number. The one she gave you."

Max read off the number and Dave dialed it into his phone. When he got an answer on the other end, he grinned. "Hi there. This is kind of an odd request, but do you have a regular customer named Angela Weatherly?" He waited. "Weatherby. Yeah, that's it. Well, I want to send her dinner. She's not feeling well and could really use some hot soup." Dave ordered the soup, then gave them his credit card number. "And can I double-check the address on that?" He grabbed a pen and scribbled the address on a notepad. "Thanks. Don't tell her who it's from. It's a surprise."

When he hung up the phone, he spun around in his chair and tossed the notepad at Max, grinning triumphantly. "She lives on Ashland Avenue in Wicker Park. They deliver to her all the time. You want her phone number, you're going to have to get it on your own."

"You should have been a detective," Max said.

"I know. I've missed my calling. And you owe me fifteen bucks for the soup."

Max stared at the address. He'd stop by tomorrow morning with breakfast, maybe a latte and a Danish. And this time, he'd make sure he got the right number. He raked his hand through his hair. "I should go."

"I thought you were going to help me clean up," Dave said.

"Another time," Max said. "I have things to do."

"You're going to drive by her place, aren't you?"

"Maybe. If the light is on, maybe I'll ring the bell and get this all straightened out tonight."

"Man, you must have it really bad for this girl."

"Yeah," Max said. "Maybe I do." He started to the door, but Dave's voice stopped him.

"Lauren called earlier. She said Mom and Dad are throwing a barbecue a week from Saturday and Mom wants you there. They've invited all their friends. I'm not supposed to tell you, but I think she has a girl she wants you to meet. She's the daughter of one of her tennis partners."

"No," Max said. "I don't need my mother finding dates for me. I'm perfectly capable."

"She's not looking for dates, she's looking for a wife for you. If you marry a Chicago girl, then you'll be sure to come back to Chicago when you retire."

"You have to tell her to stop this," Max said. "The last time I was there, she was showing me pictures of her hairdresser's daughter. She had pink hair."

"You're her baby boy. She wants to see you happy."

"I'm happy. At least for now."

"You've got one shot with this girl," Dave warned. "You better not mess it up. Court her. Woo her. Take your time and do it right."

"That's easier said than done. When I'm with her, all I can think about is dragging her to bed." He stepped out of the office and headed right for the door, his gaze fixed on the address Dave had given him.

When he got to his car, he punched the address into his GPS, then pulled out onto the street. He'd just cruise by and see where she lived. He'd be able to scope out a Starbucks in the neighborhood and make a plan for the next morning.

When he reached Ashland Avenue, he watched the GPS as it counted down the distance. Right on cue, he found the address and pulled up to the curb in front of the building. But it wasn't a house or an apartment building.

"Wicker Park Tech Centre," he read from the sign over the front entrance. This must be where she worked. It made sense. She'd work late and send out for Thai. Unfortunately, the delivery guy was going to end up taking the soup back to the restaurant.

Still fifteen dollars was a small price to pay for locating the girl of his dreams. And tomorrow morning, he'd be waiting for her.

"I JUST THOUGHT, what the hell. Why not turn those old fantasies into reality. And everything was moving along. And then he just—stopped."

"Stopped what?" Ceci asked.

"Stopped seducing me. He just stopped. He tried to make it seem like the chivalrous thing to do. He said he didn't want to ruin things between us. It was so humiliating," Angela said. "I couldn't have made what I wanted any clearer if I'd sent him an engraved invitation. Angela Weatherby cordially invites you to rip her clothes off, ravage her body and leave her gasping for more."

Angela and Ceci paused and waited to cross the street, the morning rush hour alive around them. Horns honked, brakes squealed and a bus rolled to a stop near the intersection. They walked to work most mornings. Ceci and Will's flat was only five blocks from Angela's, so they used the walk to get a bit of exercise before starting the workday.

"It's better that everything turned out this way. I couldn't maintain my journalistic integrity after sleeping with him. And, considering his frustration with the press, he wouldn't be happy to learn that I'm one of the people intruding into his private life."

"That's different," Ceci said. "You're not seeking these women out. You're not making up these stories. You're just giving them a place to vent."

"I don't think Max Morgan would see it that way," Angela countered. She took a deep breath and smiled. "So, I'm going to move on. I'll revise the chapter, choose a new subject to interview and forget I ever met Max Morgan."

It was time to put her childish fantasies behind her. After all, in sixteen months, she'd celebrate her thirtieth birthday. How pathetic would it be if she were still carrying a torch for her high school crush?

Although... Angela was certain she hadn't misread the signals. He'd wanted her as much as she'd wanted him. Something wasn't right, but she didn't know him well enough to figure it out.

"It wasn't like I have some deformity he discovered. Everything was in the right place and it looked good." She glanced down at her chest. "Maybe it was my boobs. He's probably used to really big ones."

"You have nice boobs," Ceci said. "You didn't have anything hanging from your nose or stuck in your teeth, did you? 'Cause that can really wreck the mood."

"No! I looked at myself in the mirror and I thought I looked really good. And I know I was turning him on. I mean, that much was evident. He's very well-endowed, from what I could see."

"Really," Ceci said. "You saw him naked?"

"No. He was wearing those silky basketball shorts with nothing underneath. You could see everything. And I looked—a few times—but I didn't get a chance to touch." A shiver skittered down her spine. Just the thought of Max naked was enough to set her heart racing.

This was crazy. She'd gone into this ready to

finally put Max Morgan in the past, to prove that all her fantasies were just that, silly dreams about a man who didn't exist. How was she supposed to stop thinking about him now? She hadn't slept last night at all and since she'd crawled out of bed, he'd been the only thing on her mind.

"I feel like I'm moving backward. Like I'm going back to that time when he just consumed my life. I'd lay on my bed and make up long, elaborate stories about our dream life together."

"Stop thinking about him!" Ceci said.

"Easier said than done."

"So where did you leave it?"

"He asked me out for tonight, but after what happened, I knew he wasn't going to call. If he was really interested, he wouldn't have stopped when he did." Angela smiled weakly. "And now, I can finally put him behind me, for good."

If she said it enough times, maybe that would make it true. Except, there were all sorts of beautiful memories she had of their night together. And even though it ended badly, the beginning and middle was pure heaven.

"Maybe it's better that he did stop. I mean, how would you have felt this morning if you'd slept with him last night?"

"If we'd had sex, it probably would have been incredible. Then when he dumped me, I would have been left a lot angrier than I am now."

"So what are you going to do if he calls you? What are you going to say?"

"He won't call," Angela said. "He can't. I gave him a bad number."

Ceci stopped short with a little gasp. "You what?"

"I gave him the number for the Thai place down the block from our office. See, this way, it's kind of like I dumped him. It's finally over. I've put my obsession with Max Morgan in the past and I can go on with my life."

"Well, you had one night," Ceci said in a bright tone. "That's better than nothing."

Angela's cell phone rang and her heart skipped a beat. But when she flipped it open, she noticed her mother's number. She glanced up at Ceci. "My mother. She wants me to come to Evanston for a barbecue next weekend. One of her tennis ladies is throwing it and I guess she has a son she wants me to meet. We'd be perfect for each other, she says."

Angela turned the phone on. "Hi, Mom. You're up early." She listened patiently as her mother laid out a very logical case for meeting this man, reminding Angela that the prospects for marriage were diminishing with each year that passed. It had always been a point of conflict between the two of them. Her two sisters were already married, but Angela didn't see anything in their marriages that she envied.

Both of her brothers-in-law were dull, unromantic men who didn't know half of what Max Morgan did about seducing a woman. If Angela was going to have a man in her life, he was going to be sexy and exciting and fabulous in bed. Otherwise, what was the point?

Angela held her hand over the phone. "Now, we're moving into the guilt phase. My mother knows exactly how to pull my strings."

When Kathleen Weatherby set her mind on something, there was no changing it. "Just meet him, Angie. He's a very successful fellow. He's actually a bit of a celebrity, at least your father thinks so. He plays baseball. Now I know, you might think he's some kind of arrested adolescent, but from what his mother tells me, he's made some very wise investments."

Angela stopped, grabbing Ceci's arm. "He plays baseball?"

"Yes. On some team in Florida. What was the name of that team, Jack? The Deviled…Eggs?"

"Devil Rays?" Angela asked. "He plays for the Devil Rays?"

"You know the team? Yes, that's it. Your dad says it's the Devil Rays. His name is Max. His mother and I have become such good friends and we just got to talking. He's single and you're single and it would be perfect for both of you. It's a week from this Saturday. Surely, you can fit it into your schedule."

"Mom, I really can't. I have to—"

"You cannot continue to avoid social situations

like this." She paused. "Your sisters are both happily married. Don't you want that for yourself?"

"Mom, I'm not going to marry a guy just so I can say I'm married. I'm happy. I have my work and—"

"That silly Web site of yours is not a career. You spend your whole day with all those nasty men and when a good one comes along, you won't even try."

Angela's expression must have looked worrisome, because Ceci grabbed her arm. "Just hang up," she whispered.

"I'll have to call you back, Mom," Angela said. "The reception here is really bad. Ceci and I are on our way to the office. I'll talk to you later."

Angela hung up the phone, then bent over at her waist, desperately trying to draw her next breath. "You won't believe this. This is so, so weird. I mean, it's like, spooky weird." She looked up at Ceci. "My mother is trying to set me up with Max Morgan."

Ceci dragged her over to a nearby bench and pulled her down. "Oh, my God. Angie, this is like all the karmic forces in the universe have finally converged. I was reading about this at that New Age bookstore on Damen. You can't mess with this. No matter what happens, you and Max are destined to be together."

Angela stood up. "Don't be ridiculous," she said, starting back down the street. "It's a coincidence. Don't forget, we grew up in the same town, went to the same high school. Our parents live ten blocks away from each other. They belong to the same tennis club. They'd have met sooner or later. It just happened later."

She picked up her pace. The quicker she got to the office the better. She needed to get back into her routine, work hard and put all thoughts of Max out of her head. As they approached the office, Ceci grabbed her arm again, but this time, she pulled her behind a bus shelter.

"What are you doing?" Angela asked, twisting out of her grasp.

"Look! Isn't that him?"

Angela peered through the Plexiglas wall of the shelter, then quickly turned around. "What is he doing?"

Ceci looked over her shoulder. "He's sitting on the steps, reading the paper and drinking a latte, I think. He's really cute, Angie. I mean, I thought he was cute at the bar last night. But he's cute in actual daylight. See, I told you. Karmic forces. They cannot be denied."

"Stop it. He didn't come here for me. He's probably just taking a run and stopped to rest for a bit. He doesn't know where I work."

"It wouldn't be hard to figure it out," Ceci said. "All he'd have to do is put an Internet search out for your name and SmoothOperators would come up. There was that article in the Trib six months ago. And you were on that news show in January."

"Oh, God. Maybe he's seen the Web site. Maybe

he read his profile. What am I going to do? Does he look angry?"

"Go talk to him," Ceci said. "He's sitting there waiting for you. How sweet is that? Maybe he brought you a donut. Oh, that would be so romantic."

"Why are you so determined to put us together? You're going to be the one picking up the pieces when he dumps me. And you know he will. And that's when I'm going to say, I told you so."

"Oh, boo freaking hoo. I feel so sorry for you. You have a gorgeous man who wants to take you out on a date and you're grumbling about how miserable he's going to make you. Well, don't fall in love with him then. Go out, have a nice time and see what happens. And quit being such a beeyotch or no one is going to want to date you." She paused. "Ever again."

"You're the beeyotch," Angela whispered. "And I'll hate you forever if this blows up in my face."

"I may be a bitch, but I'm your best friend," Ceci replied in a low voice. "And I love you. Now go talk to him or I will."

When Angela refused to move, Ceci stepped back out on the sidewalk and started toward the office. As she approached, Max stood up. Angela watched as they chatted for a bit, then Ceci turned back and waved at Angela. Left with no choice, Angela walked up to the pair, a smile pasted on her face.

"There she is," Ceci said, with a cheery expression. "What was wrong? Did you have a pebble in your shoe?"

"It came untied," Angela said. "My shoe." She looked up at Max. "Hi. What are you doing here?"

"He came to see you," Ceci said. "You gave him the wrong phone number last night. I always have trouble remembering my own cell phone number. I mean, you never call yourself, right? Why would you remember it." She gave Max a cute little wave, then reached for the door. "I'll see you in a bit, Angie. Don't hurry."

"What are you doing here?" Angela asked.

"I thought I'd bring you some breakfast. But I've been sitting here so long, I ate the cheese Danish and drank the latte I bought you. Do you want to walk down to Starbucks with me?"

Angela knew she could use work as an excuse to beg off. This had disaster written all over it. Even if he didn't know about the Web site, chances were he'd find out sooner or later. And she already knew the effect he had on her. When she was with Max, she forgot all the reasons she was supposed to mistrust him. Still, she couldn't help but be a little curious as to what he was planning to say. "Sure," she said.

"They won't miss you at work?"

"I'm the boss. No one will miss me," she assured him.

"Good."

They strolled down the sidewalk in the direction of the coffee shop. "You didn't answer my question," she said.

"Which one?"

"Why are you here?"

"You gave me a bogus number last night. I was wondering if you'd done it on purpose or by accident. By the way, I already know you gave me the number of your favorite Thai restaurant, so don't bother lying. That's how I found you. I sent some chicken soup to this address last night at 1:00 a.m. I thought this was where you lived."

"Chicken soup?"

"It's a long story. So why did you give me a bad number?"

Angela knew she ought to make up some excuse, but for some reason, she wanted him to know what kind of effect his behavior had on women. "I didn't want to be disappointed when you didn't call," she finally said.

"But I asked you to dinner. We had a date."

"In the heat of passion, you asked me to dinner. Things look different the morning after."

"God, you must really think I'm a jerk," he said. "And you don't even know me."

His words brought her up short. True. She didn't know him. She was lumping him in with all the other misogynists she catalogued on her Web site and wrote about in her book. And she was accepting the opinions of women she didn't know. Maybe she ought to put more trust in her own observations.

"Man, you must have dated some real scumbags to be so cynical," he said.

"No," she said. "I'm sorry. It's just that...I don't

understand why you're interested in me. I know about you, Max Morgan. I'm not your type."

"Maybe I'm looking for a new type," he said. "And maybe you're exactly what I'm looking for."

Angela smiled and shook her head. "You are smooth, I'll give you that. I'm not sure whether to believe you or to run away as fast and as far as I can."

"Give me a chance," Max pleaded. "Just one date. And after that, maybe another five or twenty. And if you don't like the way things are going, you can dump me. I promise I won't kick up a fuss."

"I'll get to dump you?"

"Yes."

She thought about the offer for a long moment. Every fiber in her being told her to refuse. She knew the danger of spending time with Max. But curiosity overwhelmed common sense. "Okay, it's a deal," Angela said, holding out her hand. "I'll give you three dates to convince me of your honorable intentions. If you don't make the grade, I'm going to cut you loose."

"Five dates," he said.

"Four," she countered.

"Does last night count?"

Angela thought about it then shook her head. "No."

"What about this morning?"

"Yes," she said.

"All right. I guess that's fair." He grabbed her hand

as they continued to walk down the sidewalk. "So, how am I doing so far?" Max asked. "Are we having fun?"

"You'd be doing better if you hadn't eaten my Danish," she said. "And drank my coffee. But I'll forgive you for that."

He grinned, then wrapped his arm around her neck and pulled her close, kissing the top of her head. "I'm glad we got this all straightened out. I was beginning to think you didn't like me."

How could she not fall hopelessly in love with this man? He was sweet and charming and funny. And he knew exactly what to say to make her feel like she was the only woman who could make him happy.

She couldn't fall in love with him. At least not completely. But a little bit wouldn't hurt, would it?

THEIR FIRST DATE WAS going well, Max mused as they sat at an outdoor table sipping coffee and sharing a cinnamon roll. He hadn't had such a simple date since…well, ever. When he dated, it usually came along with cameras and curious onlookers. Today, he felt like a regular guy, enjoying the company of a beautiful woman on a breezy summer morning.

"Tell me about your work," Max said, taking another bite of the cinnamon roll. "You said it had to do with Web design."

"I'd rather not talk about work, if that's okay," Angela said.

"You said you're the boss."

"It's only the two of us," she said. "Me and Ceci. And occasionally we have a part-time programmer working for us."

"Some of the guys on the team have their own Web sites," he said. "I never thought much of doing it myself, though. It just seems like a lot of work."

"I suppose it depends on what you want to accomplish. If you want your name to become a brand of sorts, then a Web site is a good idea."

"I don't think we have a Web site for the bar. Maybe you could help us out with something like that?"

Angela shook her head. "We really have all the work we can handle right now. But I can put you in touch with someone if you're really interested."

She glanced at her watch and frowned. They'd been sitting at the coffee shop for nearly two hours. Max had hoped she wasn't noticing the time. "It's almost lunch time," she said. "I should really get to work."

"You're the boss, right?" he asked. "Skip work for the day. Let's go to the ballpark. The Sox are playing. I can probably get us seats in one of the luxury boxes." He wasn't sure if she even liked baseball, but the word *luxury* usually appealed to women.

Angela wagged her finger at him. "I know what you're doing. You think that if you run this date into the next and then into dinner it will only count as one date," she teased.

He sat back in his hair, thoroughly amused. Man,

she just didn't let him get away with anything, did she? Most guys might call her a ball-buster, but he liked that about Angela. She kept it real. "I never thought of that. Thanks for the idea." He pulled out his cell phone and handed it to her. "Call Ceci and tell her you won't be coming in. In fact, call her and ask her to join us."

"Really?"

"Yeah, and tell her to invite someone else along. Does she have a boyfriend?"

"Will," Angie said. "He's the one who told us about your bar. He hangs out there on Monday nights with a bunch of his friends. You've met him. He took a picture with you."

"Invite him. I'll get four tickets and we'll make a day of it."

He waited while she called Ceci and when she handed him the phone back, she had a bemused smile on her face. "So this is how famous people do things," she said. "You just make a few phone calls and it's done."

"Usually," he said. "Being a celebrity is good for some things. But most of the time, it's a huge pain in the ass."

"What else could you do?" she asked. "Could you get us a table tonight at Charlie Trotter's?"

"You want to eat at Charlie Trotter's?"

"No. I'm just wondering if you could get a table there."

"Probably," he said.

"Could you get us a table at any restaurant in Chicago?"

"Probably," he said. Max knew it sounded conceited, but she wanted the truth. And maybe it was better she understood from the start what it was like to be with him. "The thing is, it can get complicated if people know where I'm going to be ahead of time. Then there are cameras and questions. Like, if we were to go sit in regular seats at the game, we'd both be in the news tomorrow. I hate that they're always in my business."

"Are you really that good a baseball player?"

"This has nothing to do with my skills on the playing field," he said. "It has everything to do with my skills playing the field."

She smiled at the joke. "It's about the women."

"Yeah, it's all about the women. Unfortunately, I realized that too late and now that's all anybody's interested in. A few months back, they wrote that I was addicted to painkillers and I was rushed to the hospital after overdosing. My nephew heard about it at school and flipped. He couldn't stop crying. They're such leeches. I hate it."

"Why would they be interested in me?" she asked. "I'm not famous."

"They're interested in anyone I'm interested in. I can't believe there was a time when I thought I wanted that kind of notoriety. I thought it would be cool to date famous women—models and actresses. Have my face in the magazines. And for a while it was pretty much fun. Unfortunately, a nice guy isn't all that interesting to the press. And if they can't find any dirt, they invent it."

"Then stop dating actresses and models," she said.

"They're going to be just as interested in you. I'm giving you fair warning. It hasn't been that bad here in Chicago. The press has kept a respectable distance. And since I told them I was thinking about retiring, I'm not such a hot story."

"Are you retiring?"

"I haven't decided," he said. "Depends upon the rehab." He paused. "Hopefully, they won't bother us. But if they do, expect that there will be some pretty silly stories."

"Like what?"

"That we're engaged, fighting, expecting a baby, hooked on drugs, dependant on booze, having plastic surgery, planning our wedding, moving to Europe, buying a mansion in Beverly Hills, looking at a condo in Manhattan, getting a dog. I don't know. It could be anything."

Angela giggled. "Wow. All that after just one date."

"It's not so funny when you're in the middle of it," Max warned.

"But we'll know what's true," she said. "It shouldn't make any difference what they say."

She was wonderfully naive about it all. And maybe she wouldn't have to endure the scrutiny of the media.

He could only hope they'd be able to get to know each other without having to deal with it.

"So, if I wanted to watch the Fourth of July fireworks from the deck of a yacht on Lake Michigan, you could arrange that?"

"Is that what you'd like to do?" he asked.

"I've heard it's really cool to watch them from out on the lake."

"I'll see what I can do," Max replied.

"I was just kidding," she said.

The fourth of July was a month away. If they were still together after a month, then it would be one of the longest relationships he'd ever had with a woman. And if Angela wanted to see fireworks from a yacht, he'd make it happen. "But today, we're going to the game." Max stood and held out his hand to her. "Now, I have to run home and change. But I'll come back in about an hour to get you and your friends."

"Where is your car?"

"At home. I ran here. I needed the exercise. Can you make it back to the office on your own?"

"No, I might get lost," Angela said, shaking her head. "I walk here all the time by myself."

"Oh, sarcasm," he said. "I like you even more now. I have a great appreciation for sarcasm." He leaned close and kissed her cheek. "I'll see you in a little while." With that, he pulled his sunglasses off the brim of his cap and slid them on. "Look both ways before crossing the street. And don't talk to strangers." He jogged backward down the sidewalk, waving to her as he went. "And prepare yourself for a great afternoon." Then he turned and headed toward home.

As he ran, he felt a wonderful energy pulsing through him. For the first time in a very long time, he was…happy. Over the past three or four years, he hadn't found much pure joy in his life. Everything he achieved seemed to come with strings attached. But this feeling he had when he was around Angela was simple to understand.

There were so many different things they could do together. The fact that she ran her own business was a big plus. They both had the freedom to come and go as they pleased. They could take off for a weekend in New York or fly down to Florida for a few days. He could steal her away to San Francisco for a romantic getaway.

As he jogged at a stoplight, waiting for the traffic to pass, Max realized he was getting ahead of himself. He needed to take this slowly. "Woo her," he said. "Court her."

But how easy would that be? The more time he spent with Angela, the more he wanted to learn everything about her—including what made her pulse beat fast and her body ache with desire. He had no doubt he could pleasure her in bed. In truth, he was much better at that than he was at dating.

"Hey, Max Morgan! Rock on!"

Max glanced up to see a truck driving by with a

kid hanging out of the passenger window. He waved and smiled. "Rock on!" he called.

The driver beeped his horn and before long, there were other drivers staring at him and waving. As soon as the light turned, Max jogged across the intersection. Though Max wanted to be a different person here in Chicago, there were always reminders that he had a different life in Florida, and a career that paid very well.

This would be a stolen summer, a time when he could experience life the way it was meant to be lived. His time wouldn't be wasted. He'd figure out the man he planned to be once baseball was over. And Angela was going to be a part of his summer. He could learn a lot from her. And maybe, if things went well, they'd have more than just this summer.

4

"WILL IS IN HEAVEN," Ceci said.

They sat together in the back row of seats in the luxury box. Will and Max were sitting outside, their arms braced on the railing as Max pointed to the scoreboard.

"Look at him," Ceci continued. "He's like a little kid." She tipped her head and fanned her face with her program. "I think I'm having a moment."

"Really?"

"How can I not love that man? He's got a pennant in one hand, a foam finger on the other and a big old mustard stain on his shirt. Who else is going to love him?"

Angela giggled. "Will is a pretty nice guy. In all the time you two have been going together, he's never done anything to make me doubt his feelings for you. There's something to be said for that."

"Max is a nice guy, too," Ceci said. "I didn't expect that. I mean, after reading his profile, I thought he'd be full of himself. But he's really sweet. And it was so nice of him to invite us here. Will is going to be talking about this for months."

"You told Will to keep quiet about our business, right?"

Ceci nodded. "Yes. And he understands completely. Besides, he's not about to do anything to mess up his chances for future fun with Max Morgan."

"Good," Angela said. "I was thinking that…well, maybe we should take Max's profile off the site. Just until…you know, we're over."

"Really? We've never done that, Angie. Don't you think we have a responsibility to be completely objective?"

"Of course," she said. "But I know how he'd feel about this. He wouldn't be happy. He'd feel like it was a betrayal."

"Well then, he shouldn't have treated those women so badly," Ceci said.

"Maybe he didn't," Angela said. "It's their word against his. And you said it yourself, he's a nice guy."

"To you. That doesn't mean he was nice to those other women." Ceci sighed. "Secrets aren't a good thing, Angie. They have a tendency to blow up in your face. Maybe you should just tell him. If he really likes you, it shouldn't make a difference."

"I'm not going to tell him," she said. "If he finds out, I'll disarm that bomb when the time comes."

They watched as Max and Will stood and walked

back into the box. They were in a heated discussion about something called a sacrifice bunt. But when they got inside, Max's attention turned toward her. He sent her a warm smile. "You having fun?"

"I am," she said.

"Me, too," Ceci replied.

Will pulled off his Sox cap, the foam finger still stuck on his hand. "Max is going to take me down to the clubhouse to meet some of the players. Is that all right? I mean, you don't want to leave right away, do you?"

"The game is over?" Angela asked.

"Yeah," Max said. "The Sox won, 4-3."

Ceci shook her head. "Nope, we're free all day."

He grinned. "Okay, then. Let's go, Max."

"Honey, you might want to clean up that mustard stain before you go," Ceci suggested.

He glanced down at the front of his shirt, then groaned. "Oh, man. I knew I shouldn't have had that fourth hot dog."

"Don't worry," Max said. "We'll pick up something for you to wear on the way."

"Right," he said. "We can do that?"

"Are you ladies interested in meeting some of the players, too?" Max asked.

"I think we'll wait here," Angela said.

Max bent close and kissed her, lingering for a long moment, before drawing away. "We won't be long. If you want anything, just pick up that phone over there and order it."

"There's plenty to eat here already," Angela said, nodding at the luxurious buffet set up along the wall. "Did you pay for all that food?"

Max shook his head. "Nope. One of my buddies on the team took care of it. My contract is up at the end of this season. I'll be a free agent and I think he wants me to come play in Chicago."

"You'd leave the Devil Rays?"

"Who knows? They might just release me if I can't come back from the injury. It might be fun to play in my hometown. At least for a year or two." He kissed her again. "Oh, and the team is called the Rays. They changed the name a few years ago."

"Oh." Angela frowned. "So there's no devil in it anymore?"

"Nope, just the Rays."

After he and Will left, she went back to sit beside Ceci. "I'm going to have to change the title of Chapter Five. He's not a Devil Ray anymore. He's just a—Ray."

"I don't think it makes much difference, do you? I mean, no one is supposed to know his identity anyway. And he is a sexy devil, that's for sure."

"I guess it doesn't matter."

"Are you really going to write about him, Angie? I think you're losing your objectivity. You wanted to take him off the site a minute ago."

She sighed softly. "I know. But despite his behavior here in Chicago, he has been the typical smooth operator. Then again, maybe he's the exception to the rule. Maybe he can change." She sighed. "The only way I can see to move forward with the book is to focus on the person he was before we met at the bar. Who's to say that he wouldn't have gone home with a different girl that night and broken her heart?" Angela reached for her beer and took a sip.

"I'm not sure what I'm going to do. He just told me he's considering moving back to Chicago to play. His contract is up at the end of this season."

"Really? So, there's a chance you could be together for a lot longer than you anticipated."

"No," she said. "I'm not going to start planning a future with him. This could all be over tomorrow. I'm not making any decisions about the site or the book or Max Morgan today. Or tomorrow."

"I hope it's not over tomorrow," Ceci said, crawling over Angela. She stood in front of the buffet. "I like being around famous people. They eat for free. They drink for free. They sit in luxury boxes and drive in fancy European sedans with tinted windows."

"I can see how fame would be addictive. Life is so easy when you have money and connections."

"Admit it, Angie. You must have imagined what it would be like to have a future with this guy. What girl wouldn't? He's gorgeous, rich, and really nice. If you're not thinking of snatching him up, then you are in serious denial."

"No, I haven't. I can't. And I won't. I'm not some silly teenager anymore. I understand the realities of relationships and what's going on here is simple infatuation. We're in that phase when we're both perfect for each other. But that will wear off. I know it will." She held up her hand when Ceci opened her mouth. "And don't go all karmic on me."

"The reality is, this guy really likes you. The way he looks at you is proof. He treats you like a princess. When he opened your car door for you, I thought Will was going to hurt himself hurrying to open my door for me. What guy in this day and age has decent manners?"

"He can have manners and still be a creep."

"Will you just give him a chance? Don't always be looking for faults. He might not be perfect for those other women, but he might be perfect for you." Ceci sighed. "Now, come over here and help me eat some of this food. We can't just leave it here. Do you think they have take-out containers?"

Angela got out of her seat and joined Ceci in front of the table. "I'm starving. I didn't want to act like I was too impressed by all this, so I didn't eat much." She paused, then groaned. "Ceci, what am I doing here? I want to hate him. I should hate him. But I can't. I feel like I'm drowning here."

Ceci nodded. "Yeah. I can see how you'd have a hard time resisting him." She popped an éclair in her mouth and considered her next words as she chewed. "Maybe you're right. Maybe he is the exception to the rule. And maybe he's been waiting for you his whole life."

Angela rubbed her forehead. "I can't think about

this now. I need chocolate. Are those éclairs?" She reached out and grabbed one, then took a bite of the custard-filled pastry. "Oh, my God. This is so good. We have to take these home. Find something to wrap them in, Ceci. I can put them in my bag."

For the next fifteen minutes, Angela and Ceci worked their way through the buffet, tasting every item at least twice. They kept an eye on the door, ready to scamper back to their seats if the boys came back. The cream puffs and éclairs and a few brownies were safely hidden in Angela's bag, carefully wrapped in a linen napkin, and the sushi rolls were nearly gone when Max and Will walked back in.

Will looked like a kid who'd just spent the day in a candy store. He showed them the baseball he'd gotten autographed and was telling Ceci about everyone he'd met, while Max stepped behind Angela and wrapped his arms around her waist. "Are you ready to go?" he asked.

"Sure." She turned around and faced him, then dropped a kiss on his lips. "Thank you for today. They both had a great time."

"How about you?"

"Me, too," she said.

"Good. Then I guess our first date has been a success. I'm batting .200 so far." He rested his hands on her hips. "I thought we could get some dinner. What about you two? Are you hungry?" he called, looking over her shoulder.

"Sure," Will said. "I could eat."

"No," Ceci said. "We have a previous commitment. We're going to have to take a rain check on dinner."

"Rain check?" Will frowned. "We don't have anything going on."

"Yes, we do," Ceci insisted. "We have that thing at that place. You know. I told you about it last week."

"You told me we didn't have anything going on today and—" He stopped short, realizing what Ceci was trying to do. "Oh, right. That thing. Now I remember." Will gave Max an apologetic shrug. "Yeah, we can't miss that thing."

"I thought you were going to tell me you had to take your mother—or was it your brother—shopping," Max said. "There's no reason for excuses. We'd love to have you come to dinner with us, right Angela?" He turned to look at her and for a second she couldn't speak. This was another moment! She was looking at Max, watching him treat her friends with such warmth and kindness and she was having a moment.

She swallowed hard. "We'd love to have you come with us," she said softly, trying to keep the emotion from tightening her throat. "I know you're not doing anything, Ceci, so don't bother making a fuss."

"No," Will said. "We'll do dinner another time. Our treat. Besides, I should check in at work. Unlike the rest of you, I have a boss who doesn't take kindly to afternoons off."

They walked out to the parking lot, chatting about

the game and laughing together like they'd known each other for years. Angela was amazed at how easily Max fit in. She'd always felt like a third wheel when she spent time with Will and Ceci, but now the wagon was perfectly balanced.

They dropped Will and Ceci at their flat and after saying their goodbyes, they got back in the car. "Dinner," Max said. "What are you thinking?"

She drew a deep breath. After everything she'd eaten that afternoon, she wasn't really hungry. And it was so hot and sticky outside, she really didn't want to get dressed up. "We could send out for a pizza," she suggested.

"I could eat pizza," Max said with a grin. "Besides, it's too hot to get dressed up and go out. Why don't we swing by your place, grab your suit and we'll take a swim?"

"The lake is really cold," Angela said.

"I've got a pool on the roof of my building. They don't allow kids, so no one ever uses it. Especially at night."

Max continued to amaze her. He knew exactly what she wanted and he'd offered it to her. She couldn't think of anything more refreshing than a swim on a summer evening like this. And pizza would be the perfect meal. "How do you do that?"

"Do what?" he asked.

"Know exactly the right thing to say. Did you take a class when you were younger? Or is there some secret handbook that they pass out to you guys?"

"I like pizza," he said. "And swimming seemed like a good idea. Would you rather do something else? Just tell me what."

"See, there you go again," Angela said. "You make it so easy for me to like you."

"Isn't that the point?" Max asked. "If I did stuff you didn't like, then you wouldn't want to go out with me."

"No, no," Angela said, shaking her head. "It's the way you do it. You make it sound like eating pizza with me is the only thing in the world you want to do."

"It is," Max said. "But if you don't want pizza, we can order Thai or Chinese. There's a really good—"

"No!" Angela cried. "It's not about what we eat."

"What is it about then?"

"If one of your buddies called you right now and told you there were some hot Swedish swimsuit models waiting for you at some bar and they were a sure thing, you'd go, right? You blow me off to hang out with them, right?"

"No," Max said, frowning.

"You're lying," Angela accused. "You would so go."

He twisted around in his seat to face her. "I would not. I'm spending time with you, because I choose to, Angie. I don't want to be with anyone else. Besides, I don't think there are many Swedish swimsuit models out there. They're too pale to tan." He turned the car on. "Now, let's go get your swimsuit and then we'll decide about dinner. What do you like on your pizza?"

This was exactly what she expected of him. With absolute ease, he could make her believe she was the most important woman in his life. That his entire world revolved around her. And that eating pizza next to a pool with her was better than dining at a gourmet restaurant with a movie star.

She knew the sexy devil was charming. But she'd never realized just how insidious that charm could be. With every moment they spent together, she was more convinced Max wasn't the man with the profile on her site.

She wanted to throw her arms around his neck and kiss him until her lips were sore. She wanted to run her fingers through his hair and smooth her palms over his chest and discover the body beneath the clothes.

Was it so wrong to want him? Why not admit she'd been taken in, just like all those other girls? Why not enjoy it while it lasted? Angela knew the risks of surrender, but right now, looking into his gorgeous eyes, the rewards far outweighed any risk to her heart.

THE UNDERWATER LIGHTS cast wavering shadows on the pool deck. Max sank below the surface then swam underwater to the opposite end, popping up in front of Angela. Bracing his hands on either side of her legs, he boosted himself up and kissed her before dropping back down into the water. "Are you going to come in?" he asked. "It's really nice."

"I'm having more fun watching you," Angela replied with a wicked grin. She swirled her feet around in the water in front of him and he grabbed her foot, kissing the arch. "It would be much more fun if you didn't have those shorts on."

Max glanced up at her, his lips pressed against her ankle. "What would be the point if you won't get in the water. I won't let you drown. I promise."

"I'm not worried about that," she said.

"What are you worried about then? I've already seen you wet and you look beautiful with your hair all stringy. Unless you don't want to get that suit wet."

She wore a pretty flowered two-piece that left just enough to the imagination. It was the first chance he'd had to really appreciate the beauty of Angie's body. She was fit, not thin, with curves in all the right places. Unlike a lot of the girls he'd dated, she boasted no surgical enhancements. Her breasts, her nose and her lips were all completely natural.

Angie leaned back and stared up at the sky, kicking her feet in the water. "This is so nice. It's like we're not even in the city anymore. I can't believe people don't use this pool. I'd be up here every night."

"It would be more fun if it belonged exclusively to us," he said. "I have a pool at my place in Florida. Bigger than this one." He kicked off the side and swam toward her. "With a hot tub. And a big, tall fence around it."

"I have bathtub," Angela teased. "I do laps every morning."

"All right," Max said. "That might have sounded a bit egotistical. Maybe I was hoping to impress you." In truth, he was thinking about how much fun it would be to take off his shorts and her suit and enjoy the feel of her body against his in the water. If they were in Florida, he wouldn't have to worry about anyone barging in on them. After swimming for a while, they could lie down on one of the comfortable chaises on the deck and continue what they'd started in the pool.

Max pulled himself out of the water and sat down next to her, pushing aside the fantasy. "You're very hard to impress."

"That's not true," she said.

"What do you like about me, Angela?"

She regarded him with a cool stare, her eyebrow arched. Max had never met a woman like her before. She certainly kept him on his toes. He wasn't sure from one moment to the next what she was thinking. But then, when she turned that smile on him, he could almost believe she was as captivated by him as he was by her. "I like your…hair," she said, lowering her gaze in mock innocence. "And you have a very nice body. And your voice. That's nice, too."

"Nice?" He jumped back down into the pool, then pulled her along with him. She cried out in surprise, but he held tight, cradling her body against his. "I told you the water was nice."

"It's warm. Like bathwater," she said. Angela wrapped her arms around his neck and kissed him, deliberately taking her time before drawing away. Her body rubbed against his provocatively and Max wondered if she knew what she was doing to him. "I like your mouth," she said. "And the way you kiss me."

Max growled softly as he pulled her into another kiss. Beneath the water, her skin felt like silk. He ran his palms from her shoulders to the small of her back, then drew her hips against his. "What about the way I touch you?" he asked.

"I like that, too," she whispered. "See, there's a lot about you that I appreciate."

Something had changed. The moment she'd kissed him, he felt her grow pliant in his arms. A silent surrender. He slipped his hand between them to cup her breast, softly teasing at her nipple through the fabric of her suit. Angela watched him, and then to his surprise, she reached back and untied the top, letting it fall in front of her.

Max bit back a groan. It took every ounce of his will to resist. But she'd given him an invitation to touch. How could he refuse? Sinking down further, he traced a line of kisses from her shoulder to her breast. And then, his mouth found her nipple, peaked from his caress.

Angela moaned, tipping her head back and

furrowing her fingers through his hair. Max pulled her legs up around his waist as they bobbed in the water, his lips gently exploring the exposed flesh. But as he continued, Max knew they were reaching the point of no return.

He drew back and waited until she opened her eyes and looked at him. "Are you hungry? We could go down and order the pizza."

Angela sent him a puzzled looked, the same one she'd given him that first night when he'd stopped mid-seduction. "No. Let's stay up here a bit longer. It's so relaxing." She undid the back of her suit and tossed it on the deck, then closed her eyes and leaned back, holding her arms out until she floated in front of him, her hair fanning out around her. He moved his palm up her belly, then back again.

It was so easy to get caught up in his desire, Max mused. Though he tried to ignore his need to possess her, there were moments when he let himself imagine what they might share, what it would feel like to move inside her. He'd always followed his instincts, taking pleasure where it was offered without any regrets.

But what had seemed so casual with women he barely knew, took on much more meaning with Angela. He wanted her, not to satisfy his own needs, but so that he might know everything about her. The impulse to strip off the rest of their clothes was too intense to ignore.

She opened her eyes and he pulled her back into

his arms. "I'm hungry," he murmured. "We should go down."

Confused, Angela watched him for a moment, then reluctantly nodded. He slipped his hands around her waist and set her on the edge of the pool, then crawled out next to her. Straightening, Max helped her to her feet and collected the towels he'd brought with him, wrapping one beneath Angie's arms to hide her naked breasts.

They rode the elevator down three floors to his twenty-second floor apartment. When they opened the door, the chill from the air conditioning rushed out.

"You should get out of that wet suit," he said softly, his gaze fixed on her mouth. Max rubbed her arms and her skin prickled beneath his touch. "I'll get you something warmer to wear."

She stared at him, silently, as if she were waiting for something more than words. "Here we are again," she said. "With just a towel between us."

"I don't—"

"The last time we were in your apartment, you were wearing it." She reached down and slipped out of the bottom to her suit, letting it drop to the floor before kicking it aside.

This was crazy, Max thought. They were both consenting adults. Why wait any longer? And she was right. All it would take was just a flick of his finger and the towel would be gone. He reached down, smoothing his hand over her shoulder. "You really want to do this? I can wait."

"Why are you waiting?" she asked.

"I don't want to mess this up," he said. "But if you really want—"

Angie nodded. "Yes, I really want this. Do you?"

"Oh, God, yes," he said.

A moment later, the towel fell to the floor and she stood in front of him, naked. Max wasn't quite sure what to do first. He picked up the towel and rubbed it over her body. He'd never denied himself before, never even considered the consequences of indulging in recreational sex. But it was different now. He needed this to be right between them.

She grabbed the towel from his hands and began to rub it over his chest. Then she hooked her finger in the waistband of his board shorts. "You should get out of your wet suit," she murmured.

He slowly shoved the shorts down over his hips, then let them fall to his feet. Drawing a deep breath Max waited, allowing her to make the next move. She made work of drying him off and every time she came close to his growing erection, he held his breath. There was no ignoring the fact that he was aroused, but she was doing a pretty good job of it.

When she finally tossed the towel aside, Max slipped his arm around her waist and pulled her body against his. The contact was everything he'd expected it to be, electric and overwhelming, so powerful that he thought he might come before she even touched him.

With nothing between them, they were both free to explore each other's body and they did, slowly, silently, each caress a tantalizing prelude to the next. There was nothing of the practiced seducer in him anymore. He wanted to proceed at her speed, making sure that his pleasure was secondary to hers.

The distance that she usually kept between them was suddenly gone, dissolving the moment her naked body touched his. She arched into his touch, her breathing quick and shallow, her lips searching for his. And when her fingers finally grazed his rigid cock, Max was ready to explode.

He clenched his jaw and drew a deep breath, thinking about the embarrassment he'd suffer if he let himself go to soon. The thought was enough to temper his need.

Slowly, she stroked him, her touch soft, but firm, and he grew even harder beneath her caress. Max pressed his lips into the curve of her neck, listening to her soft gasps and tiny sighs. And when he finally touched her between her legs, the gasps turned into a moan of such intensity that he thought she'd reached her peak already.

He stopped, then began again, this time his caress more gentle. If they only had one night together, it would be the best night she'd ever experienced. He'd bring her to an orgasm so powerful that she'd never forget it. So powerful that she'd want to experience it over and over again.

ANGELA KNEW SHE WAS CLOSE. His gentle assault sent wild sensations coursing through her body. She could barely form a rational thought, yet she was almost afraid to let go.

If she did, everything she'd ever thought about him, every negative stereotype she'd attached to him, would be gone. She'd never be able to think of him without remembering this. He wanted her, needed her as much as she needed him. This wasn't just a casual seduction; they shared something between them, something special.

A current flashed through her body and suddenly, she was there, on the edge again. Let go, her mind screamed. Surrender and everything will be all right. But could she trust that he'd be there to catch her?

A slow ache built inside of her, a tension she could no longer deny. Casting caution and common sense to the wind, Angela surrendered, her mind completely focused on the feel of his fingers between her legs.

The first spasm hit her hard and by complete surprise. She cried out, grabbing his shoulders to maintain her balance. When the shudders came, she jerked away, unable to take it anymore. But he was there again, drawing her orgasm out, making her give him every last bit of her soul.

When it was finally over, she leaned against him, her legs weak, her body completely spent. She'd never experienced anything so powerful before. Angela closed her eyes and felt the tears well up in her throat. If she was wrong about him, if this was the end instead of the beginning, then she'd regret this night for her entire life.

"Are you all right?" he whispered.

She nodded, her cheek pressed against his chest. "I think so."

"Would you like to continue or do you want to rest for a while?"

She pressed a kiss to his chest, amused by the question. "I think I can continue."

"Good," he growled, scooping her up into his arms. He carried her down the hall to his bedroom, then dropped her onto the bed, stretching out on top of her and trapping her body beneath his, his hands braced on either side of her head. "You know that once we do this, we're going to want to do it again. And again."

"I'm counting on that," Angela said.

He bent his elbows, his mouth hovering over hers. "Are you ready?"

"Yes," Angela murmured.

He kissed her, his lips soft against hers, his tongue tracing the shape of her lower lip. As she lost herself in the tantalizing taste of his mouth, he reached down and pulled her leg up beside his hip. Angela knew that with just one shift of her body, he could be inside of her. But she was willing to wait, allowing Max to choose the moment.

As his mouth drifted over her body, Angela closed her eyes and enjoyed the fresh rush of need that pulsed through her veins. Though the after-effects of her orgasm still controlled her responses, she felt a new desire begin to grow inside her.

Again and again, he brought her close, with his fingers, with his tongue, until she was whispering his name, pleading for relief. When she tried to finish it herself, he gently drew her hand away and then began again.

When she finally couldn't take any more, he sensed her need. Before she could open her eyes, he had retrieved a condom from the bedside table and sheathed himself. She waited, arching against him as he settled between her legs. And then he was there, softly, slowly entering her, inch by delicious inch.

Angela held her breath, the pleasure so intense every nerve in her body was on fire. Max began to move, drawing away and then driving into her in a languid rhythm that betrayed his own desire.

She looked up at him and he smiled sleepily, his eyes drifting shut with each thrust. Her pleasure only intensified and she was surprised at how quickly he brought her back to the edge again.

Her fingers dug into his shoulders as she urged him on, deeper and faster, bringing her closer and closer. And then, to Angela's astonishment, another orgasm wracked her body. But this time, he was with her, tensing, then shuddering as he thrust deep and hard.

When it was over, Max kissed her softly, nuzzling

his nose against hers. It had been everything she'd dreamed it might be and so much more. Maybe Ceci was right, Angela mused. Maybe this was some kind of karma. They seemed to fit together so perfectly, as if they'd been made for each other.

He lay down beside her, his hand clutching hers, his gaze fixed on the ceiling. "I'm really, really hungry." His stomach growled and he pulled her hand up and kissed it. "Sorry. There are just certain parts of my body I can't control."

Angela turned over and patted his belly. "We can order pizza now."

"Pizza will take too long. I want something sweet," he said. "Not that your body wasn't delicious, but I need carbs right now if we're going to do this again."

"Are we going to do this again?" Angela asked.

"Damn right we are," he said, sitting up. "Do you think we could send out for ice cream? Does Dairy Queen deliver?"

"No," Angela said. "But I have another idea. Go get my bag. I think I left it next to the door."

He crawled out of bed and Angela watched as he walked out of the room, admiring his wide shoulders and tight backside. He really did have an incredible body, so perfect. Except for the surgical scar on his shoulder, he could pass for one of those Greek statues. She wondered how many other women had admired his butt from the seats of various baseball stadiums.

When he returned, Max set the bag on the bed. "Please, tell me you have a candy bar in there."

"Nope. Do you have milk? We need milk."

He left again and Angela pulled out the desserts she'd pilfered from the stadium. Spreading the napkins on the bed, she rearranged the miniature cream puffs and éclairs and frosted brownies on the napkin, then waited for him to return.

When he did, he stopped at the door of the bedroom, staring at the feast laid out on his bed. "I've never understood the mysteries that lie at the bottom of a woman's bag, but I won't question this one."

Angela patted the spot beside her. "Sit."

He handed her the half-gallon of milk and she set it down beside her bag. "Is there a fully-equipped pastry kitchen in your purse?"

"No, I took these from the table at the ball game. They were just going to go to waste and they were so good."

He tipped his head back and laughed. "I swear the surprises never end with you, Angela. And just when I think I have you figured out."

"What's surprising? That I'd steal goodies for future consumption? I'm a very practical girl, Max. You should know that by now."

"That you'd admit it with such unabashed glee. Besides it's not stealing when it belonged to you in the first place. It's relocating. Or even liberating. You liberated those éclairs."

She picked one up and held it out to him. "Taste."

Max bit into it and then moaned softly. "These are good."

"Better than sex?"

Max pretended to consider his answer, furrowing his brow. "Better than bad sex. Doesn't touch what we have, though. That would take a double chocolate cheesecake with raspberry sauce and whipped cream."

Angela pretended she was insulted, then playfully pushed an éclair into his nose, leaving custard dripping onto his chin. But before he could return the favor, she leaned forward and caught the dripping custard with her tongue. Slowly, she licked the rest of the mess off his face.

"Do that again," he murmured.

Angela straddled his crossed legs, facing him, the éclair in her hand. She touched the chocolate to his nose, then licked it off. Dotting custard and chocolate on different parts of his body, his shoulder, his chest, his biceps, she used it to explore the perfection of his form.

When she was through, she took a huge bite of the éclair and handed it to him. "Yum," she said with a wicked grin.

"Now I'm all sticky," he said.

"We could go back up to the roof for a swim."

"That sounds like a plan," he said. "Or we could just take a shower."

She lay down next to him and groaned. "I love éclairs but I don't think they love me." Angela rubbed her belly. "Let's stay here a bit longer. I'm not sure my legs are fully functional yet."

He grabbed the milk and took a long drink, then set it aside. "I could get used to this," he said.

"Eating éclairs in bed?"

"No, having you in my bed. Naked and happy. I like it."

Angela smiled to herself. She'd expected to feel a tiny bit of guilt over what they'd done, a sliver of doubt over her choice. But there was nothing about what happened between them she could regret.

"I guess our second date went pretty well," he said, staring up at the ceiling again. "Swimming, sex and dessert. My batting average is quickly rising."

She reached out and smoothed her hand over his belly, coming to rest at his groin. "You've got a few more innings left to play, Max," she said.

5

MAX ROLLED OVER IN BED, opening one eye to the morning light. A sharp pain in his shoulder caused him to curse and he rolled back again, working out the twinge. Though the surgery had been nearly four months ago, he still had pain. Either the swimming or the sex had been too much for him and considering how much time he spent at both last night, Max was sure it wasn't the swimming.

When the ache had subsided, he sat up and found the other side of the bed empty. "Angela?" he called. His voice echoed through the silent apartment. Then he noticed the note on her pillow. Max snatched it up. "I have to work sometime. Date number two tonight. Better make it good."

He chuckled, then flopped back down onto his pillow. Smiling seemed to be the only thing he could manage. His body was exhausted, his desire completely sated and he felt completely transformed. He reached for the phone beside the bed, ready to call her, merely to hear her voice. Then he realized he didn't know her number by memory yet.

At that very moment, the phone rang and he reached out and grabbed it. "You better have a very good reason for leaving my bed this morning," he said.

"Some of us have to work," Angie replied. "And with all the noise I made, you didn't even move. You were snoring."

"I'm sure that was attractive," he said. "What time did you leave?"

"About an hour ago. I caught a cab. I just got home. I'm going to shower and then head into work."

"Why don't you shower and head back here?" he said. "You're the boss, you can take the day off."

"I took yesterday off," she said. "And if the boss doesn't work, the boss doesn't make money."

"I have plenty of money for both of us," Max said.

"I'm not dating you for your money," she said.

"Why are you dating me?" he asked.

"For your body. Call me later. Tonight, I get to choose what we do. Go back to sleep."

"Bye, baby," he said.

"Bye," she cooed.

The line went dead. He switched off the phone and tossed it aside. But almost immediately, it rang again. "She can't get enough of me," Max murmured. He pushed the button and held it to his ear. "I knew you'd change your mind. My bed is so lonely without you."

"That is not what a mother wants to hear first thing in the morning, Max."

He winced, biting back a curse. "Hi, Mom."

"Hello, darling. I won't bother asking you what you've been doing."

"It's not what you think," he said.

"I prefer not to think about it," she said. "Get out of bed and get dressed. I'm on my way to your place. We're going to have coffee. I'll pick you up out front in five minutes."

Max ran his hand over his chest. He was still sticky from last night's adventure with the éclairs. "Give me ten. I have to hop in the shower."

"All right. I'll see you in a few minutes." Max drew a deep breath and rolled out of bed. Reaching behind his head, he stretched the kinks out of his shoulder, then rubbed at the scar as he walked to the bathroom.

Five minutes was all he needed for a shower and five minutes after that, he was downstairs, watching for his mother's car. When the Saab pulled up, he hopped in the passenger side, then leaned over and gave his mom a kiss on the cheek.

"Where's the nearest coffee shop?" she asked.

"Out the driveway, then take your first left. As long as we're in the car, we'll go to my favorite place."

Max gave her directions as they drove west. The coffee shop, Beanie's, was in a busy part of the

Lincoln Park neighborhood. He kept his eye out for a parking place, but knew that at this time of the day, it would be a while before they found something close. To his surprise, his mother pulled into a spot a few moments later.

"Why is it I can search forever for a spot and you always find one the minute you start looking?"

"You're buying me coffee," Maggie Morgan said as she stepped out of the car.

"It's free," Max said. "I own this place."

"Really?" She stared up the facade. "It's very nice. So you feed them drinks at night and soothe their hangovers in the morning. Your father would call that smart business." She walked past him. "Too bad you don't conduct your personal life with such care."

"Here we go," Max muttered. All of this because he'd made a mistake answering the phone. He followed his mother inside, then ordered coffees and pastries for them both. They found a table near the window and he pulled out her chair for her. "Before you start in on me, I'll just say that the woman I was with last night is someone pretty special."

"Movie star or model?"

"Neither. Just a regular, normal girl. Well, not normal. Very pretty. And nice. You'd like her."

"Maxwell Morgan, it is time you seriously reevaluated your social life. You can't keep sleeping with these women and expect any good to come of it. You're not going to find a nice girl that way."

"Oh, I know what this is about," Max said. He took

a bite of his pastry and slowly chewed. "David told me you want to set me up on a date. That's why you're here. To convince me to come to your barbecue. I'm not interested. I'm busy that weekend."

"Just consider this girl. She's lovely and she's from a good family. And she's not the sort to go sleeping around."

"You've met her?"

"No, but her mother has shown me photos. She owns her own business and has a master's degree. You went to high school with her. You might even remember her."

"I went to high school with 3,000 kids," Max said. "I didn't know all of them."

"She went to Northwestern, too. Although she finished all four years." His mother grabbed her bag. "I brought your yearbook along. We'll look her up and see if you remember her." She flipped through the pages. "Here she is." She paused. "Oh, my. This isn't a very flattering picture. She looks nothing like this anymore." She slammed the book shut. "Just trust me. Besides, if you don't hit it off, you haven't lost anything."

Max grabbed the yearbook. "Show me. I'd like to know what you consider a lovely girl."

Reluctantly, she found the page again and then held it out to Max. "Top row, second to the last."

"Where?" Max asked, scanning the photos.

"There," his mother said. "She had braces and

she's wearing glasses. She looks so much better now. She's blond. You seem to prefer blondes."

The photo looked strangely familiar, but he shook his head. "Oh, Mom, no. This girl I'm dating is really great. I was thinking about bringing her to the barbecue. Her name is Angela."

"Yes, dear. Angela Weatherby. I know."

Max blinked in surprise. "How did you know that? Did Dave mention her?"

"It's right there, next to the photo."

"What?" Max shook his head. "What photo?"

His mother pointed to the list of names in the yearbook. "Angela Weatherby. That's her name. Kathy Weatherby is my tennis partner."

Max stared at the picture for a long moment, dumbfounded. If he squinted his eyes, he could almost believe this was the woman who'd shared his bed last night. He bit back a curse. What the hell did this mean?

When they'd met, Angela had acted as if they'd been strangers. How could she have gone through four years of high school without— No, everyone in school knew who he was. And that wasn't just ego talking, it was the truth. He'd been class president his junior year and student body president his senior year.

His brain scrambled to make sense of it. What had seemed so simple last night was suddenly incredibly complicated. Max had to question Angela's motives and rewind every comment she made. Was this part of some clever manipulation?

Some of his buddies in the league had some experience with stalkers. Was Angela one of those? He slowly worked through the events of their short time together. No, she'd given him a bogus phone number. Why would she do that? Unless she knew his interest would be piqued and he'd come looking.

And she had been evasive about her background. She'd never mentioned where she went to high school or college. "Can I keep this?" he asked.

"Of course. Now, you'll be coming to the barbecue, right?"

"Yes," he murmured, his gaze still fixed on the photo.

"Alone?"

"Yes," Max replied. "I'm very anxious to meet this girl. There's something very familiar about her. In fact, I feel as if I know her quite…intimately." He stood up. "I have to go, Mom."

"But we've barely started our coffee."

Max bent over and gave his mother a kiss on the cheek. "I have a lot of things to do today. Don't worry, I'll walk home."

"All right," she said. "I'll see you a week from Saturday. Come about one. And wear something nice. I hate seeing you in those silly basketball shorts all the time. Wear a shirt. In fact, buy a new shirt. Then send it to the cleaners to be pressed. And no jeans. Khakis."

"Are you going to pick out my underwear for me, too?" Max asked.

"You don't have to be snippy," she warned.

"Sorry. I'm tired."

"I just want you to be happy," she said, her expression softening.

"And that's all I want for you, Mom. I'll be at your barbecue. I promise." He walked out of the coffee shop and onto the busy sidewalk. For a long moment, Max wasn't sure what he wanted to do. He wasn't even sure how he felt. Angry? Confused? Shocked?

He pulled his sunglasses down and headed east, toward the lake. "Let's review," he murmured. "I didn't know her, but she knew me...maybe. We went to high school and college together, but we never—" He cursed softly. "We might have met." There was a reason he'd thought he knew her that first night. They had met. But when?

"Think." He'd only been in college for two years. She probably hadn't looked much different from her high school graduation picture, with the exception of the braces. And maybe the glasses. She'd told him she'd been the president of the Latin Club. Max stopped and paged through the yearbook until he found the photo. "There she is," he murmured. "Angela Weatherby. President."

This was all too strange. Like it had all been planned out ahead of time. He'd known women— baseball groupies—who'd gone to great lengths to meet him, but was Angela one of them? Had she walked into the bar that night hoping that she'd catch his eye? The groupies he'd encountered were much more obvious about their intentions. Unless she was so good at manipulating men that she knew how he'd react if he were forced to chase her.

Max needed some straight answers. Now. But he wasn't even sure what questions he ought to be asking. It would be better to wait and let things between him and Angela play out. A few well-timed questions about high school and college might shake the truth out of her. And then he'd know if this was a complicated manipulation or just a simple misunderstanding.

Max hoped it was the latter. Right now, he didn't want to consider anything that might mess up the good thing they had going.

"I LOVE THIS PLACE," Angela said, staring into the penguin tank at the Shedd Aquarium. "Whenever I need to clear my mind, I come here and watch the penguins. Life seems so perfect for them. Swim and eat, swim and eat."

She glanced over at Max, her gaze taking in his perfect profile. They'd been together for two days and she'd done her best to resist his charms. But his constant assault on her defenses had left her feeling exposed and vulnerable.

It was just sex, incredible as it was. But it was the simple moments like this one, when she'd look at him and saw the man behind all the hype and celebrity that threw her. He was just a regular guy who loved pizza and swimming and watching penguins. He was completely content to spend a quiet afternoon with her.

"They're like us," Max said. "But we threw a little sex in there for variety."

"Penguins mate for life, you know."

"I didn't know that," Max said.

"It's true. They search for that one special penguin they're meant to be with and when they find each other, they settle down, build a nest and have a little penguin family."

It was only after she relayed the penguin information that she realized how he might interpret her words. Did he think that's what she was after? Was she even sure what she wanted? Angela had been so careful not to think about the future. Whenever her thoughts spun out to the weeks and months ahead, she stopped herself.

Two days. Forty-eight hours. And already she was in serious trouble. It wasn't going to last, Angela told herself. In a week or two, he'd give her some sort of lame explanation and he'd move on. Why not just enjoy what they shared for what it was?

"It must take them a while to find their mate," Max said. "They all look alike."

"They know. They can feel it." He looked at her and Angela smiled. "They stick together through sickness and bad weather, protecting each other. From the time they meet until the time they hatch their first baby, they don't even eat. And then, the couple shares all the responsibilities for the newborn."

Max slipped his arm around her shoulders and they silently watched the birds leap into the water and jump back out again. If only life could be so simple for humans. She'd already made so many mistakes and now, Angela wasn't sure she'd be able to go back and fix them.

How would she explain everything to Max—how she'd been in love with when they were teenagers? How she'd once dreamed about a day when they'd be doing just this. How she'd decided to write about him in her book and how his personal life was splashed all over her Web site.

No matter how she fashioned her explanation, she could never make it sound better than common stalking. But it wasn't like that. What had begun as a complicated mess was now perfectly simple—she wanted him, he wanted her, and they'd found each other.

If she really believed they had a future together, then she'd have to come clean. The barbecue would be difficult to navigate with all her secrets still intact, so she'd have to tell him before then. Either that, or break up with him.

"What do you think about that?" Max asked.

Startled out of her thoughts, she blinked, then turned to him. "Think about what?"

"About mating for life? Is it possible?"

"Of course. Zoologists have studied penguin colonies and—"

"I meant for humans. Is it the natural order of things to spend your life with just one person?"

"I don't know," she said. "Look at the divorce rate nowadays. All those couples went into marriage thinking it was forever. And then it wasn't. Relationships are hard. I think two people have to be temperamentally suited for each other. And then they have to work at it, every day, forever."

"Have you ever thought about getting married?"

"No one has ever asked me," Angela admitted. "But I do believe in the penguins. I think there's one person out there for each of us and we spend our life trying to find that person. Sometimes, we think we've found them, and then we realize we were wrong. But when we actually do, it's...perfect." She forced a smile. "And what do you think? Are you a believer in the penguin theory of love or do you side with my parents?"

"Your parents don't believe in romance?" he asked.

"They think I need to choose someone to marry for practical purposes, not because of some overwhelming passion. I was the oddball in our family. My parents and sisters were the scientists, always looking at life with a purely objective, rational eye. I spent my whole childhood lost in silly romantic fantasies. I loved fairy tales. My mother thought they were horrible stories that sent young girls all the wrong messages. She banned certain books from my reading list and I'd just sneak them out of the library with my best friend's library card. She wouldn't allow me to read Wuthering Heights because Cathy commits suicide over her love for Heathcliff."

"Do your parents have a happy marriage?"

"No," Angela said. "Maybe. I don't see any passion there. I know they respect each other, but I was never really sure if they loved each other. What about yours? Are they happy?"

Max nodded. "Yeah, I know they are. They have their disagreements, but they love spending time together. They golf and play tennis. And I'm pretty sure they still have sex, so that's a good thing, right?"

"I think so," she said. "I hope that when I'm older, my husband still wants me."

"You want to get married, then?" Max asked.

She shrugged. "I don't know. I suppose if the right man comes along."

"And the perfect guy. He would be…"

Angela laughed. "You want a list? I don't know. He'd be honest and kind. Funny. I think humor is important."

"Rich?"

Angela shook her head. "No. I'd want him to be passionate about his work, but money isn't a deal breaker. I guess that's it. Honest, kind and funny. And maybe spontaneous and romantic, too." She frowned. "It doesn't seem like much. I really should have found a guy by now, don't you think?"

"Maybe you're like that penguin right there," Max said, pointing to the tank. "Maybe you're still searching."

She slipped her arm around his. And maybe she'd found him already and was just too stubborn to acknowledge it, Angela mused. "Let's go get some lunch. And then I have to get back to the office. I've been taking too much time off work and leaving everything to Ceci. It's really not fair."

"Do you ever take a vacation?" Max asked.

Angela shook her head. "Not really."

"Then why don't we go somewhere this weekend, just the two of us."

"I don't know," she said. "Maybe next weekend?" If they were both out of town next weekend, then neither one of them could attend the barbecue. "I'd have more time then."

He shook his head. "That doesn't work. I've got plans. My parents are throwing a barbecue." He paused. "You wouldn't want to come with me, would you?"

"No!" Angela quickly replied. "I mean if I'm in town, I should probably get some work done."

"It's probably for the better," Max said. "There's this woman they want me to meet. The daughter of one of my mother's friends. I'll just go and say hello."

Angela's breath caught in her throat. This was where her real life intersected with the life they'd created for themselves. She risked a sideways glance, trying to read his expression. Was it possible that his mother hadn't mentioned the name of this woman? "So you have a blind date?" she asked. "What's her name?"

This was it. The truth was about to come out, right here in front of the penguin tank. Angela was glad. She hated all of the secrets between them. She'd make her explanations and if he couldn't except them, then it would be over.

He paused, then shrugged. "I don't know. She went to high school with me, but I don't remember her."

Relief washed over her. He didn't know it was her. Though the urge to tell him was still there, Angela decided to take more time to consider her approach. She loved the penguin tank and didn't want one of her favorites spot ruined by a bad memory.

"She can't possibly be as beautiful as you," he said.

Angela felt guilt snake through her. Did he know? Had Max already figured everything out? This was her fault for hiding things from him in the first place. She should have walked into the bar and admitted her reasons for being there. If she had, she certainly wouldn't be stuck in this mess now. No, considering his hatred of the press, he probably would have tossed her out on her ear.

"I wouldn't be so sure about that," Angela said. She'd tell him at lunch. She'd confess everything and then let the chips fall. If he was still in her life at the end of the day, then they might actually have a future together.

"DATE NUMBER THREE," he said. "Let me see. Penguins at the aquarium, a long swim, take-out pasta for dinner, and early to bed. I think I deserve top scores, don't you?"

Angela nuzzled her face into his shoulder, her naked body pressed against his. "You're getting awfully confident. You expect top scores for take-out pasta?"

"It was from a great restaurant. Face it. You like me. You think I'm hot. I'm irresistible. I managed to talk you out of going back to work, didn't I?"

"You're not that irresistible," she said.

She'd been awfully quiet since they'd left the aquarium. Max knew what was on her mind. She was trying to work up the courage to admit that she'd known him all along. His first impulse was to attach some ulterior motive to their meeting at the bar that night. But after he thought about it for a while, Max realized that there might be another reason she didn't want to admit their common past. She'd been one of those girls that nobody noticed in high school, the girls who watched from the sidelines. The girls that a guy like Max wouldn't have bothered to talk to.

Max ran his hand along her body, cupping her backside and pulling her up to lie on top of him. All that had changed. And not because she was beautiful, but because he had finally found a reason to see beyond mere physical beauty.

This stolen summer had changed him. He'd grown up, become an adult. And he was finally beginning to realize what life was all about. It wasn't about money or fame. It was about this—the small, perfect moments that he shared with Angela. The quiet conversations and long silences. The simple kisses and the passion that followed.

"I am irresistible," Max said, searching for her mouth. His lips brushed against hers and he moved above her, his shaft growing harder between them. "Admit it."

"No," she said. "I can resist. Just watch me."

Her wicked smile was an outright challenge to him. And though they were only teasing, Max suddenly needed her to acknowledge what was happening between them, the power that their attraction generated. Did she want him as much as he wanted her? How deep did her feelings run?

Their conversation at the penguin exhibit had given him a few clues. She wanted a relationship, something that would last, even though she hadn't come right out and said it. And wasn't that what was going on here? A relationship?

With all the other women in his life, he saw their time together in finite terms, with a beginning and an end. But he wasn't able to contemplate ending things with Angela. Though she hadn't been completely honest with him, her actions certainly weren't enough to drive him away. In truth, he felt even more attracted to her knowing how vulnerable she felt about her past.

Still, there were two sides to every relationship. What would drive her away? Would it be his celebrity? The long periods apart? Her past? There were plenty of things on his side of the board that she might find unbearable.

Max pulled her into a long, deep kiss, doing his best to seduce her with his lips and tongue. "Say it," he whispered. "Tell me you need me."

"I don't," she said, still teasing.

Max took her face between his hands and stared into her eyes. "Tell me," he said.

She paused, clearly confused by the intensity of his request. Then she drew a ragged breath. "I need you," she murmured.

"Only me," he said.

"Only you," she replied. Her smile widened. "Unless you have someone else under the covers. Another man? Oh my, a threesome. I suppose I could spread the need around."

It was clear she wasn't about to engage in a serious conversation. And maybe it wasn't fair of him to press her. After all, they'd only known each other forty-eight hours. What did he expect?

"I have something for you," Max said. "In the envelope on by the lamp."

"What is it?"

"Open it," he said.

Angela shook her head. "We shouldn't be giving each other gifts. It's too soon."

"It's not really a gift," Max said. "Just open it."

She grabbed the envelope and slowly withdrew the airline ticket. "It's a ticket," she said. "Are you going somewhere?"

"I have to fly to Florida tomorrow and I was hoping you'd come with me. We could spend the weekend there. I could show you the city, then we could relax and have some fun."

At first Max thought she'd accept, but slowly her expression changed. "We talked about this earlier. I—I can't."

"Why not? It's just a couple days. I want to show you where I live."

"I just can't," she said. She rolled off him, grabbing his T-shirt from the end of the bed and tugging it over her head. "I—I'm going to go get some orange juice. Do you want some?"

Max pushed up on his elbow. "Angela, wait."

"I'll be right back," she said, forcing a smile.

He watched her walk out of the bedroom, then flopped back on the pillow. What was this all about? He thought she'd enjoy a little vacation. Since he had to be in Florida for a few days, why not take her along? There was something else at work here.

When she returned, Angela sat down at the edge of the bed. "I'm sorry," she said. "It's a lovely…gift."

"No, it's not a gift. Jewelry is a gift. This is just me being selfish," Max said. "I have to be away for a few days and I knew how much I'd miss you. I thought if you came along, I wouldn't miss you so much." He reached out and touched her arm. "Is that so bad?"

She shook her head. "Not really." Angela took a sip of the orange juice. "But that's your other life. Down there, you're famous, you have girls and paparazzi trailing after you. I can't compete with that life. It's so…big. But here in Chicago, everything works."

"Angela, I might have to go back to that life. It's my job. What's going to happen then?"

She shrugged. "I don't know. We'll deal with that when the time comes, I guess."

"I want to know now," he said.

"We've known each other for—how long?"

"Forty-eight hours," he muttered.

She blinked in surprise. "Really. That's all? I've had stomach viruses that have lasted longer than that. I've had headaches that have lasted—"

Max pressed a finger to her lips. "I get it. But you forget, we've spent nearly all that time together. If you were dating some other guy, you might have had dates that lasted for five hours max."

"Yeah," she said.

"Right. Well, we've had the equivalent of…" He tried to do the math in his head. Nine times five was forty-five so—

"Nine point six," she said. "I'm good in math, too."

"All right. We've been on the equivalent of 9.6 dates. Now, if you figure two dates a week, we've been dating for almost five weeks. Five weeks is not too early to take a trip together."

"It's too early for me," she said.

Slowly, it became clear to Max what she was saying. "You don't trust me," he said. "Go ahead. Say it. You don't trust me."

"I don't trust you," she said. "And not because you're not a great guy. I don't trust you because I barely know you, Max. And I don't trust myself. I don't want to get hurt. I don't want to see the wonderful life you lead in Florida. I don't want to be reminded of the differences between us."

Differences? Damn it, they'd grown up in the same hometown, attended the same schools. Their parents were friends. If she were going to use that as an excuse, then he'd have to call her on it. Or maybe that was the reason she'd kept a few secrets from him. After dating starlets and pop stars, what could he possibly find interesting about a hometown girl?

"Forty-eight hours," she repeated. "That's barely enough time to figure out how you like your coffee."

"You know how I like my coffee," he said.

"And it doesn't help that we spend most of our time in bed. I know a lot about your body and about how you like to be touched. But I don't know how you got that scar on your knee."

"Bike accident when I was twelve," he said.

"Or what you like to read," she added.

"Mostly non-fiction." He sighed. "All right. I get

your point. So, let's get to know each other right now."

"I'm still not going to Florida with you," she said.

"I know you're stubborn," Max said.

"Cautious," she countered.

He bent close and kissed her. "And your lips are incredibly soft."

"You're getting off track again," Angela warned.

Max cupped her breast in his hand. "And that your body seems to fit perfectly against mine. As if it were made for my touch."

She sighed softly. "Why don't we play a game? I'll ask you a question—any question—and you have to answer. We each get ten questions and two passes."

"Passes?"

"We can refuse to answer twice. I'll start."

"All right." Max sat up and crossed his legs in front of him, then pulled a pillow over his lap. "Shoot."

"How many women have you slept with?"

He laughed. "Really? You want to know? I'm not sure I ever counted, but it's not as many as you'd think."

"More than five hundred?"

"No," Max said. God, his reputation must be a lot worse than he'd ever imagined. "Where did you hear I'd slept with five hundred women?"

"More than two hundred?"

"Absolutely not," he said.

"More than one hundred?"

Max shook his head. "I don't think so. I've had some long dry spells and I've had some short-term relationships. Maybe ninety." He paused. "Jeez, even that sounds like a lot. But it's really not. If you figure ten on average a year. And that's since the beginning. A lot of what you hear in the press isn't true. If it were, I'd be up in the thousands. How many questions was that for you—four?"

"No, just one."

"Actually, it was four. One main question and three sub-questions."

With an astonished laugh, she reached out and slapped him on the chest. "You don't play fair."

"My turn," he said. "Same question."

"None," she replied.

"None?"

"That's question two according to your rules. And my answer is none."

"You've slept with me, so it has to be at least one."

"Oh, but you're a man. You said same question. So I answered the same question—how many women have I had sex with."

He grabbed her and threw her down on the bed, stretching out on top of her. "Oh, so this is the way it's going to be. You're going to trick me. I might as well give up right now. You're much too clever, Angela Weatherby."

"All right, all right, no more tricks."

For the next two hours, they talked, asking

questions, laughing at answers, and learning more about each other than they needed to know. Max carefully avoided questions about her hometown and her high school and college education, waiting for her to volunteer that information herself. And though she had plenty of opportunity, she never once mentioned she'd known him in the past.

When it came time to ask his last question, Max paused. "I think I'm going to save it," he said.

"For what?"

"For later. For when I really want to know something."

"I can always pass on it."

"No, you can't. You've had your two passes, re-member?" Max pulled her into his arms and kissed her. "Now, can we please just stop talking and start getting down to business?"

She growled playfully, then grabbed his face and kissed him long and hard. "Max, if kissing is your business, then I think I'd like to invest."

6

ANGELA SAT AT HER DESK and stared at her computer screen. As hard as she tried, she couldn't seem to concentrate on work. Max had been gone for two whole days. He'd called a few times, but their phone conversations had been stilted and short, like two strangers trying to find something interesting to say to each other.

He hadn't been sure when he was going to get back and though she'd been anxious to see him again, she didn't want to press him on the matter. She'd tried her very best not to want him too much, but the effort was taking a toll on her heart and her body.

"Look at this," Ceci said. "Someone posted another comment on Max. SunkissedGrl goes into great detail about how he charmed her, then never called her again."

"It didn't take him long," Angela said.

"You don't think he went out with this girl this weekend?" Ceci said.

"He could have," Angela said. "How do I know what he's been doing? He could be having an orgy down in Florida for all I know."

"Angie, you need to accept the fact that this guy might really like you. You can't automatically think the worst of him."

"Why not? What makes me different from all those other girls? He's here in Chicago for the summer. Obviously, he wants to find someone to…seduce. Why not me? I was handy, willing." Angela moaned, burying her face in her hands. "And stupid. I was stupid."

Ceci reached out and rubbed her arm. "No, you weren't. You just led with your heart instead of your brain."

"And now, I'm falling in love with him. After just a few days together. I try to stop these feelings but I can't. It's like I'm sitting on the Metro tracks and there's a big train coming and I can't move. All I can do is wait for the impact."

"There's nothing wrong with falling in love," Ceci said. "Sometimes you have to take a risk."

"But don't you see how ridiculous this is. I'm doomed to fail, yet I can't help myself. When he finds out about the Web site, he'll hate me. When he finds out we went to high school and college together, he'll mistrust me. And when he finds out I'm falling in love with him, he'll run away as fast as he can."

"You don't know that. He may be the exception."

"Stop saying that!"

"You just assume everything will fall apart," Ceci said.

"It's much easier than thinking about a real future with Max." She paused. "I can't believe I just said those two words in the same sentence. Max. Future. Sometimes this does seem like a dream."

"It's real. I was at the ballgame. He was there. In the flesh."

A shiver skittered down Angela's spine. Putting the words *Max* and *flesh* together created a brand new flood of sensation. "I can't think about him right now," she said. "It's making my brain hurt."

Angela picked up her cell phone. She'd checked it at least a hundred times already that day. "Stop it," she scolded. "I feel like some silly teenager. I was this silly teenager, mooning over him, wondering where he was and what he was doing every minute of the day." She stood up. "I have to go home."

"We could get some lunch. Eating always takes your mind off your worries."

Angela shook her head. "No, I'm not hungry. Maybe I need a nap. I haven't really been sleeping the last few nights."

"Nothing to tire you out?" Ceci asked.

"Right." Angela forced a smile. She grabbed her bag and threw it over her shoulder. "I'll see you tomorrow."

"Tomorrow is Sunday. Will and I were going to drive out to—"

"Sunday," Angela said. "I knew that. Monday, then."

She stepped out into the heat of a Chicago summer day, the street busy and the sidewalk crowded with pedestrians. Angela walked to work most days and had done it so many times that she could find her way home with her eyes closed.

She stopped at the grocery store and picked up a deli container of chicken pasta salad. At the last minute, she bought a bottle of wine. Maybe a few drinks would put her mind at rest and allow her to sleep.

Angela walked home slowly, her thoughts focused on Max. She'd been thinking about him all day, waiting for him to call, wondering why he hadn't. Of course, she could have called him. There wasn't anything improper in that. They were sleeping together. The rulebook had been burned the moment they tore off their clothes and jumped into bed together.

She reached into her bag and searched around for her cell phone, then checked again to see if she had any messages. "What does this mean?" Angela murmured. Was this how it would end? He'd just stop calling and move on to another girl?

As she turned the corner and approached her flat, she noticed a BMW sedan double parked on the street. Angela's heart skipped a beat. It couldn't be him. Just wishful thinking. He would have called to tell her he was coming back.

She slowly approached and when she was beside

the car, the passenger-side window lowered and Max leaned over the seat, a wide grin on his face. "Get in," he said.

"You're back. Why didn't you call?"

"I did. Three or four times. And I just called the office. Ceci said you were on your way home."

"You called? I didn't get any messages."

"Something's wrong with your cell phone," he said. "Come on, let's go."

She reached for the door. "Where are we going?"

"Away," he said.

"How far away?"

"I thought we'd drive up to my cabin and spend a few days," he said. "It's not a vacation. Just a long drive with a bed at the other end. And a lake. And a boat."

This time, Angela wasn't about to refuse. He'd been gone for two days and she'd barely survived his absence. Another two days apart and she'd be ready for the psych ward. "Shouldn't I pack some clothes?"

He shook his head. "You won't need any. And if you do, we'll buy them on the way."

Angela stared at him for a long moment. This was exactly what she'd always wanted from a man—excitement, spontaneity, romance. How was it possible to go from the depths of doubt and despair to this, all in the course of a few minutes? This is exactly why people ended up going crazy over love. "You just want to leave, right now?"

"Yeah," he said, waving her inside. "Let's get out of the city and have some fun."

She opened the door, then hopped inside the car. "All right, let's go."

Before long they were racing north through the sparse Sunday traffic. Inside the cool interior of the sedan, soft music played beneath their conversation. He was back and it was as if he'd never left. Everything was exactly the same between them.

Yet everything that she'd gone through in the past few days wasn't that easily forgotten. Angela couldn't imagine surviving another separation without a better understanding of how he felt about her. She drew a deep breath and turned to him. "What's going on with us?" she said.

He glanced over at her. "What? We're going to my cabin."

"No, I meant, with us. You and me."

"Oh, no," he said, shaking his head.

"I just asked a question," she said. "I mean, we're dating, I know that. But are we exclusively dating? Would you be angry if I told you I went out with another guy while you were gone?"

"You went out with another guy while I was gone?" he asked, his brow arching in surprise. His jaw twitched and his gaze remained fixed on the road.

"No. Did you go out with another girl?"

He shook his head. "No."

"So...we're dating."

"Exclusively," he said.

"You could say we're having a...relationship?"

"Yes, you could say that," Max replied.

"Would you say that?"

He nodded. "Yes, I would say we're having a relationship. It's a little weird at times, but it's interesting."

Angela sank back into the leather seat and smiled. "All right."

He reached across and slipped his hand around her nape, furrowing his fingers in her hair. "Feeling better?"

"Absolutely," she said. "I'm glad we got that cleared up."

"THIS IS AMAZING," she murmured. "It's so beautiful. And quiet. It's hard to believe Chicago is only four hours away."

Max handed Angela a glass of wine, then drew her over to one of the Adirondack chairs on the porch. "Sit," he said.

She shook her head. "No. Let's walk down to the lake. We can sit on the pier."

"All right," he said. He laced his fingers through hers and they strolled down the steps to the dirt path that led to the water. "I haven't spent much time up here since I bought the place six years ago. My brothers come up and fish a few times each summer. And my sister brings her kids up, but the place is closed most of the time."

She drew a deep breath. "I love the smell. The trees and the lake."

"You act like you've never been on vacation," he said.

"I haven't," Angela said. "I've traveled for business. And I spent the usual semester abroad. But, until recently, I didn't have the money for a real vacation."

"You've never gone on vacation with your family?"

She shook her head. "Not a relaxing vacation. When my family vacationed, it was always a teaching opportunity. We visited museums and historical sites. I can't tell you how many times we've been to Washington, D.C. We never just sat on a beach and relaxed. My parents believed that sitting around was a waste of time."

"We had the best vacations when I was a kid," Max said. "We'd all pile into the family van and we'd just go. Four kids, my parents, and the dog. We'd camp and hike and cook over a open fire and spend as much time as we could outside."

"Sounds nice. There were times when I seriously wondered if I'd been adopted. I never fit in with my family. My two sisters and I are so different."

"How?" he asked.

They sat down at the end of the pier and stared out at the setting sun. "They were so focused in everything. From the moment they exited the womb, they had a plan. My parents were so proud."

"They weren't proud of you?"

Angela laughed. "Sure. But my parents never really knew who I was. I pretended to be one thing for them, but inside I was different. I was a dreamer. I lived in my own little world. When I was a kid, I didn't have just one imaginary friend, I had a whole roomful of them. An alternate family, with brothers who took me horseback riding and sisters who loved to play dress-up."

"What's wrong with that?"

"My parents and sisters don't have any imagination. I used to think my name was magical and that's why I was so different. I was like an angel. My sisters are Susan and Mary. Very practical names. But my name was…romantic."

"I like your name. You look like an angel."

Angela laughed, remembering his attempts the night they met. "And you are so full of it, I can barely tolerate you," she teased.

"You don't take compliments well at all."

"I'm not used to them. My parents never complimented us. We were expected to be confident and self-possessed. We weren't supposed to need coddling." She paused. "I love my parents, don't get me wrong, but sometimes I think I could do a better job raising a child."

"I think you're perfect just the way you are," he said. "And if you ever need me to tell you that, you just speak up." Max kissed the end of her nose. "Do you want to go for a swim?"

Angela shook her head. "I'm hungry. Maybe we can make some dinner first?"

Max stood up and grabbed her hand, pulling her to her feet. As they walked up the rise to the cabin, he lagged behind her, taking in the view. "You have a very lovely ass, too," he said.

She turned and looked at him, a bemused smile curling her lips. "Don't think that's going to get you anywhere, buddy," she said.

He caught up with her, grabbed her around the waist and tossed her over his shoulder. "We'll see about that," he said.

When they reached the house, it only took them a few seconds to strip off the clothes they wore. Max lifted her up on the kitchen island, his lips wandering over her body. She was perfect, every inch of her a delicious revelation.

This was exactly how he imagined weekends at the lake. A little wine, a little conversation and a lot of sex. He'd just never found the right companion, until now.

"I'll bring the cooler in. It's too heavy for you!"

The sound of his brother's voice shocked Max out of his haze of passion. Angela jumped, then quickly slid down beside Max. A moment later, the screen door opened and Dave and his family bustled inside.

A tiny scream burst from Angela's throat and Max

cursed beneath his breath. They both dropped down to the floor, their heads poking above the countertop. "Ah, Dave?"

His brother glanced over into the kitchen, then stopped. The kids and Lauren ran into him from behind. "Max? There you are. We saw the car. What are you doing up here?"

"I could ask you the same."

"We thought we'd come up for a few days. Lauren doesn't have to work on Monday and Tuesday, so we wanted to take a long weekend. I thought I told you."

"Why is Uncle Max hiding?" six-year-old Brittany asked. "Can I play, too?"

"If you don't want your kids to get an eyeful, I think you'd better take them outside," Max warned.

"Everybody out." Dave and Lauren quickly hustled back out the door and a moment later, the cabin was silent.

"Oh, no," Angela moaned. "This is not the way I imagined meeting your family."

He turned to her. "You've imagined meeting my family?"

"No! I was speaking generically. Do you think they saw anything?"

"No. But I'm pretty sure Dave and Lauren have a good idea what was going on. And it wasn't hide and seek."

"Go get my clothes," she whispered. "I'm staying right here."

Max hurried out to the living room and gathered everything up in his arms, then returned to the kitchen. The clothes went on more quickly than they'd come off and when they were both fully dressed, he grabbed her hand and pulled her toward the door. "Come on, I'll introduce you."

Angela dug in her heels. "No. I don't want to meet them. Not right now."

"They'll be fine."

When Max got to the door, he pushed it open. Angela shook her head, but followed him, stepping outside. The kids were already down at the lake with Lauren and Dave was sitting on the porch steps. He stood when he saw Angela.

"Hey, I'm sorry," he said, holding out his hand. "I'm Dave, Max's very rude older brother."

"This is Angela," Max said.

"Weatherly?" Dave asked.

"Weatherby," she said. She glanced at Max, a questioning look in her eyes.

"Dave helped me track you down after you gave me that bogus phone number. You really made an impression on him."

"I'm going down to the lake and introduce myself to your wife and children," Angela said. She walked down the steps and followed the path across the lawn.

"I didn't see anything," Dave called to her. "I swear."

Max jabbed him in the ribs with his elbow. "Don't make it worse than it already is."

"I lied," Dave muttered. "I got an eyeful. But don't tell her that. And for God's sake, don't tell Lauren. By the way, that girl has got a nice body. She's the first naked woman I've seen since I've been married. I mean, except for pictures in magazines. And porn."

"If you don't shut up right now, I'm going to kick the shit out of you," Max warned.

"Okay," Dave said. "I just never thought you'd be up here. When we saw the car, I figured we'd have a nice family weekend."

"I do own the place," Max said. "Is it so difficult to believe that I might want a little privacy?"

"Of course not. But I just assumed you'd be in the city." He picked up a football from the pile of toys he'd brought along and tossed it up in the air. "Hey, go out for a pass."

"I'm not in the mood," Max said. He had been in the mood for sex until a few minutes ago. The interruption had made things a bit uncomfortable for the moment.

"Come on," Dave said. "Don't be a pussy. I'll take it easy on you. You won't hurt yourself."

Max trotted across the lawn for twenty yards, then caught a perfect spiral from his older brother. Though Max had played football throughout high school and his first year of college, he'd never liked it as much as baseball. He did remember how to catch a ball, though. "Nice," he called.

"Throw it back," Dave said.

Without thinking, Max heaved a pass, then realized he probably shouldn't be stressing his shoulder outside of his rehab exercises. He rubbed the spot just beyond his collarbone, surprised there'd been no pain.

"You all right?" Dave called.

"I'm fine." Frowning, he walked over to his brother. "It didn't hurt. In fact, it felt good. Strong. It hurts when I wake up in the morning, but after I warm up, it feels pretty good."

"What did the team doctors say?"

"They did an MRI and a few other tests. They said it's healed and I can start to throw again. I just have to start real easy."

"Hey, that's great," Dave said, clapping him on his back.

"Yeah," Max murmured.

"You don't sound thrilled. How come?"

He shrugged. "I guess I just assumed it wouldn't come back, that I wouldn't have to make a decision about going back. That the decision would be made for me. But now they're saying I could start training with the team again mid-July if everything goes well."

His stolen summer would be over before it really began. He'd have another month with Angela and then they'd go their separate ways, at least until the end of the baseball season.

Max grabbed the football and started toward

the water. When he'd come to Chicago for rehab, he'd mentally moved on with his life. Once he'd met Angela, a future without baseball seem even more attractive.

He sat down at the edge of the water. A moment later, Dave joined him. "You want to tell me what this is all about? I thought you were determined to get back in the game."

"I was. Not so much anymore."

"Is it the girl?"

"Her name is Angela. And she's not just one of my girls. She's different."

"I can see that. But you say that about every girl you date."

Max cursed beneath his breath. "This time, I mean it. I can see myself with her...for a long time. Maybe even married to her."

"What do you know about her? You've been together, what? A week? Maybe you ought to check her out before you fall in love," Dave suggested.

"What do you mean? Like, hire a private investigator?"

"It couldn't hurt, Max. You've got a lot of money. You need to make sure she's interested in you for the right reasons."

"You never suggested this with any of the other girls I dated."

"Because those relationships were doomed from the start. But you really seem to like this girl."

"Woman," Max insisted. "She's not a girl, she's a woman."

"I can arrange for it," Dave said. "I work with a firm that does background checks on our bartenders. It's a simple process."

Max shoved the football into Dave's lap and stood up. "Nope, there's no need. I've got everything under control."

He walked along the pier toward Angela. Everything wasn't under control. There were still a lot of questions that needed to be answered. And he was running out of patience.

ANGELA PICKED A CARD, then showed it to the two girls. "Blue," she said. She moved her Candyland marker to the next blue square. "I'm winning. You better watch out."

Brittany grabbed the next card. "No, it's my turn," Bethany cried.

"She's right," Angela said. She glanced over at Max and he smiled at her, then cocked his head toward the door. Angela nodded and a moment later, Max squatted down next to the coffee table. "I'm going to steal Angela away for a little while," he said. He held out his hand and pulled her to her feet. "Come on. We're going for ice cream."

"Me, too!" Bethany cried, scrambling to her feet.

"Take us. We wanna go," Brittany added.

"No, it's late," Max said. "And it's almost bedtime

for you two. We'll go tomorrow, I promise. But tonight, Angela and I want to go by ourselves."

"I bet they're going to get naked again," Brittany whispered as she and Bethany walked off.

"Mama says they weren't naked. They had their swimsuits on."

As they stepped outside, Max slipped his arm around her shoulders. "We may have scarred them for life." When they got up to the driveway, Dave's SUV was parked behind the BMW. Max pulled her along to the road. "We'll walk into town. It's only a mile. And it's a nice night."

The winding road through the woods was quiet, with only the occasional rabbit or squirrel to interrupt the silence. "My family used to come up here when we were kids. We'd rent a place on the other side of the lake. It was just a small cabin. My folks would stay inside and we'd get to sleep in tents. I tried to buy the place when I was looking, but the family that owned it didn't want to sell."

"This place is nice," she said.

"I remember how much fun it was up here, the freedom we had. My folks would go to bed early and we'd be out until all hours of the night, prowling around in the woods, playing in the water, walking into town."

As they approached town, the sky grew a bit brighter from the lights. The ice cream stand was a beacon in the dark, neon outlining the facade. The parking lot was crowded with cars and kids. "We came here for ice cream almost every day. Back then a cone was just fifty cents. The place hasn't changed at all. What do you want—cone or bowl?"

"Bowl," Angela said.

"Chocolate, vanilla or strawberry?"

"Strawberry," Angela said. "With just a tiny bit of chocolate on the side."

Max nodded. "I learn something new every day. I would have pegged you for a pure chocolate girl." He walked up to the window and placed their order. A few moments later, he returned and they found a seat at a table beneath a tall maple tree.

"This is nice," she said, licking a bit of ice cream off her spoon.

"It's nice to be alone again. I feel like we haven't been able to talk all evening. I'm sorry about Dave and the kids showing up," Max said. "I had no idea they'd be here."

"It's not a problem. I kind of like it. It's a real family vacation. Lauren was saying that she was happy to see you using the place. She said the family likes having you around."

"Tell me more about your family," he said. "Where did you grow up?"

The question seemed to come out of nowhere and Angela coughed, a blob of ice cream catching in her throat. Suddenly, a blinding headache pierced her temple. "Ow," she said. "Brain freeze."

Her discomfort distracted him for a moment and

Max reached out and rubbed her forehead. "Just breathe real deep," he said.

When the ache subsided, she took another bite of her ice cream, letting it melt in her mouth. "Around Chicago. The suburbs."

He stared across the table at her, his spoon poised in midair. "Which suburb? There are so many."

She glanced up at him, trying to read the odd expression on his face. Did she really want to spoil this wonderful weekend with a fight? "Does it make a difference?"

"Yes," he said. "I think it does. This is my last question, Angie. The one I was saving?"

Angela took a ragged breath. He knew the answer already, she could see it in his eyes. Somewhere along the line, he recognized her, remembered her or simply figured out she was hiding something. "You know, don't you? You know exactly where I grew up."

Max nodded. "Yeah. I do. You're from Evanston. We went to high school together. And college, at least for the two years I was there. And you know that next Saturday we're supposed to meet at a barbecue?"

Angela nodded. "At your parents' house. Your mother and my mother are tennis partners. My mother called me the day after we'd met to invite me."

"A little strange, isn't it?"

A tiny smile curved the corners of her mouth.

"But you don't remember me, do you. Don't worry, I wasn't very memorable. I blended into the walls."

He stood up and they started their walk back to the cabin, still eating ice cream as they strolled. "Why didn't you mention this when we met?" Max asked. "Why weren't you just honest with me?"

She sent him a sideways glance, wondering how honest she ought to be. There was a bit more to her story than just a high school crush. "Maybe I wanted you to think I was beautiful and alluring and a little bit mysterious. Maybe I didn't want you to remember the plain, nervous girl I used to be."

"I wouldn't have remembered that girl. We'd never met."

"But we have," Angela said. "A number of times."

"When?"

"You bumped into me during freshman orientation for high school. You said sorry, and then walked away. And once, I handed you a book you'd dropped in the library. And you sat in front of me for a whole semester in physics class."

"That's it?"

She shook her head. "I once interviewed you for the college newspaper. It was right after they started scouting you for the pros. You'd just done that calendar for the athletic scholarship fund."

"Oh, my God, that's it," Max said. "That's where I knew you from." He reached out and pulled her into his arms. "When I saw you at the bar that night, I felt as if we'd met before, but I couldn't remember when. That was it."

"There was one other time. A few years ago. I was at a sports bar in Evanston, waiting for a table and you were there. And…you looked at me. Across the bar."

An odd expression, and then one of slow realization crossed his face. "I remember that. I remember how I felt when you looked away. There had been this connection and it shocked me. I'd never had that happen before. Not since then, either." He paused. "That was you?"

"That was me," she said.

"I should have introduced myself. I was tempted, but I was with—"

"Another woman," she said. "Several, I think."

"My sister," he said. "I think Lauren and Dave were there, too. It was around Christmas and I was home for the holidays."

"It's probably better you didn't come over. I would have babbled something stupid and you would have walked away wondering who'd let me out of the asylum for the night. I would have been that stupid, silly girl who watched your every move and went home at night dreaming about kissing you."

"What?"

Now that she had the opening, Angela didn't want to stop. It was time to tell him everything. Or almost everything. "You might as well know the rest of the story. I had a crush on you in high school. And in

college. In fact, that's why I went to Northwestern.
I was supposed to go to Sarah Lawrence, but when
I heard you were going to Northwestern instead of
straight into the minors, I followed you there. I know,
it sounds pathetic, and it really was."

Max stared at her, his gaze fixing on her mouth.
She wanted him to kiss her right then, to reassure her
that nothing had changed between them, to put a stop
to her clumsy explanations. In all the moments they'd
shared over the past week, she'd never felt quite so
vulnerable.

"A crush?"

"I suppose this changes everything," Angela said,
her voice trembling with emotion. "I'm not the person
you thought I was. I'm not exciting or interesting or
even the tiniest bit mysterious. I'm just a girl from
your hometown who was once hopelessly infatuated
with you."

"How long did the crush last?"

"I don't know. Six years. Then you went into the
minors and I decided to move on."

"So, you were in love with me and I was just going
about my life without ever knowing you had these
feelings? You were watching me and dreaming about
me and hoping I'd talk to you and—"

"You can stop now," Angela said. "I'm going to
crawl off into the woods and die." Now that she'd
completely humiliated herself, she needed the conversation to move to a new subject. "This is really
good ice cream. The sign said it was custard. What's

the difference between ice cream and custard? I never could figure that out."

"And that night, in the bar, when we met," Max continued. "That was it. That was probably the last chance for us. If I hadn't come over to talk to you, you would have left and we never would have met."

"Well, there's always your parents' barbecue," she said.

"I would have found an excuse not to go," Max replied.

He seemed a bit stunned by her revelation, by the series of coincidences that had brought them together. Angela knew she ought to continue, to tell him about the Web site and the interview for the book, but he'd already been given too much to absorb. Maybe tomorrow.

Max drew a deep breath, then nodded. "I guess we were lucky."

"How is that?"

"I was lucky. To have finally recognized what I'd been missing all those years."

A blush warmed her cheeks. He didn't seem angry, or offended, or deceived, just…bewildered. A bit amazed. "You're not angry that I wasn't honest from the start?"

Max shook his head. "Nope. Hey, I know I have a reputation. Maybe if you'd admitted everything up front, I might not have been…intrigued. But you have me now. And you're stuck with me."

Tears swam in Angela's eyes. "Really? You're not

going to dump me because I'm Angela Weatherby, former Evanston High School wallflower."

Max hooked his finger beneath her chin and drew her closer, then dropped a kiss on her lips. "As long as you don't drop me because I'm Max Morgan, former jackass and serial seducer from Evanston High School."

"Deal," she said.

"So I guess we've told all our secrets and we're officially in a relationship," Max said.

She swallowed hard. "I guess so."

Max dipped his spoon into her ice cream. "You know that means that we can share our ice cream. Can I have some of your strawberry?"

Right now, Max could have anything he wanted, Angela mused. Her heart, her soul, her body. Everything she wanted to believe about him was proving true. He was kind and honest and romantic. And she was falling in love with him all over again.

7

MAX PACED BACK AND FORTH in front of the fireplace. The night was warm and all the windows in the cabin had been thrown open to catch the breeze. Outside, the trees rustled and he could hear the gentle lap of water on the shore.

He loved nights like this, when everything was so still. He glanced over at the rack that held a selection of fishing poles. He could sit on the end of the pier and fish, but Max suspected that it wouldn't put thoughts of Angela out of his head. They'd be leaving for Chicago in the morning and he wanted to share this place with her, to show her what her life might be like with him in it.

Instead, they'd been sent off to separate bedrooms, for the sake of the children. Angela was in one room with Brit and Beth while he'd been given another room with Davey, his three-year-old nephew. Of course, Dave and Lauren took the big bedroom, with the comfortable bed, the bed Max should have been sharing with Angela.

Max opened the closet and pulled out a pair of sleeping bags and set them next to the door. If they couldn't sleep together inside the cabin, then they'd sleep together outside.

He walked down to the pier and tossed the sleeping bags into the boat, then jumped down into the cockpit. The aft seat folded out into a comfortable lounge, almost as wide a bed. He unzipped the sleeping bags and laid them out, then surveyed his work in the pale moonlight. It wasn't the Ritz, but it was certainly better than what they'd been given.

If Max had had his way, they would have driven back to Chicago as soon as Dave and Lauren arrived with the kids. But Angela had insisted on staying and she seemed to enjoy the time with his family, even if it meant playing endless games of Chutes and Ladders and Candyland with the girls.

Now that they were officially in a relationship, family would probably become part of the picture and strangely enough, Max didn't mind. He hadn't introduced a girl to his family since his senior prom date in high school, but he felt reasonably certain that Angela would be in his life for more than just a few months.

As he walked back up to the cabin, he contemplated the possibility that he'd met the girl he was going to marry. Max had always thought once he found her, everything would fall into place. He never considered that he might have to convince her to take a chance on him.

When he walked back inside, he headed for her bedroom. Max knocked on the knotty pine planks, but the knock was met with silence. Was she already asleep? He knocked a bit louder and a moment later the door opened. She looked at him through sleepy eyes. "What are you doing? You're going to wake the girls," she whispered.

"What are you doing?" Max asked, his gaze taking in her pretty face and tumbled hair.

"Trying to sleep," she said. "But it's impossible. They keep wriggling around every time I close my eyes. They're all arms and legs. Between the lumpy mattress and their elbows and knees, I feel like I'm being assaulted."

"If you come and sleep with me, I'll be much nicer," he said.

She peeked out the door. "Where are we going to sleep? On the floor?"

"Come on. Come with me." He reached out and grabbed her hand, pulling her along through the dark cabin. When they reached the door, he pulled her into his embrace and they stumbled out onto the porch, caught in a desperate kiss.

He furrowed his hands through her hair and molded her mouth to his. It had been at least two hours since he'd last kissed her. "I don't like sleeping alone."

"You weren't alone."

"I didn't have you there. That's alone."

"Where are we going?"

The moon was nearly full, lighting the way for part of their escape, before disappearing behind a cloud. Though the air was still warm, there was a damp breeze coming off the lake. Angela shivered and Max slipped his arm around her shoulders, pulling her close.

They hurried down to the pier, then laughing softly, stripped off their clothes and jumped in the water. Though the air was chilly, the water was warm. Max stood on the sandy bottom, his arms wrapped around her naked body, his face nuzzled into the curve of her neck. "Someday, I'm going to steal you away to a deserted island. Just you and me. No one else."

"Why?"

"I just want to see what it would be like to be completely alone with you," he said. "With no distractions or interruptions."

"We're alone now," she said.

Max looked out across the lake. In the distance, a light from a motorboat was visible, slowly skimming across the water. He furrowed his hands through her hair and pulled her into a fierce kiss. "Do you know how difficult it is being around you without touching you?" he asked, sliding his hand over her breast. "I like being able to do this whenever I want."

Angela sighed softly. "I like it, too. I like falling asleep with you and waking up with you. And swimming naked with you."

His lips found her breast and he teased her nipple to a peak. She shivered and he pulled her closer. "The very first time I kissed a girl, I was sitting on a pier on the other side of the this lake." Max pointed to a light across the water. "The white light to the left of the blue one. We met on that pier and I kissed her."

"So this is where it all began?" Angela asked.

"I guess you could say that. God, I was so nervous I thought I was going to throw up. I didn't know what to do with my hands. I wasn't sure where to put them."

"I see you've figured that out," she teased.

"I remember how exciting it was. My heart was pounding so hard, I thought it would burst out of my chest." He kissed her again. "Kind of like now."

"I was a junior in college before I got my first kiss," Angela admitted.

"Really? How can that be? You're so damn kissable."

"I was a very late bloomer. As you know, I lived in a fantasy world throughout my teen years, dreaming of this gorgeous baseball player I knew."

"I feel bad," he said. "I wish I'd have known you back then."

Angela shook her head. "No. You would have thought I was just pathetic. I wouldn't have been able to put together a coherent sentence. Believe me, it's much better that we met now."

"I guess so," he said. "So, when did you bloom?"

"Are you asking me when I first had sex?"

"Yes."

"You answer first."

"Well, surprisingly late. I fooled around a lot, but I didn't want to do anything that might mess up my future in the major leagues. It was the summer after I graduated from high school. She was the older sister of one of my teammates. After that, there was no going back. What about you?"

"I was twenty-one. By my junior year in college, I'd decided it was time to put a little effort into my appearance. I tossed aside the ugly duckling and tried to become a swan. And it worked. Sort of."

"It sure did," he murmured.

He kissed her again and when he drew back, he fought the urge to tell her exactly how he felt. Whether he wanted to admit it or not, he was falling in love with Angela. By tomorrow night, they'd have known each other a week. He was already imagining what it would be like to know her for the rest of his life.

"Are you cold?"

"It's a little chilly out here."

"I've reserved a private room for us." He pointed to the boat. "It's got a beautiful lake view, a nice big bed and all the privacy we could want." He helped her back onto the pier and then held her hand as she stepped down into the boat.

He grabbed a towel and dried them both off,

admiring the sight of her naked body in the moonlight. Then they crawled beneath the sleeping bags and pressed their naked bodies together for warmth. "What do you think?"

"I've never slept outside before."

"Never?"

She shook her head. "What if I have to go to the bathroom?"

"You walk back up to the house," he said.

"But aren't there animals outside?"

"Wake me up. I'll come with you."

She drew a deep breath, then relaxed. "No pillows?"

"Do you want a pillow?" Max asked.

"Yes, please. And a bottle of water. And my lip balm. I left it on the beside table in the bedroom."

"We're supposed to be roughing it," Max said. "I don't think lip balm and bottled water qualify."

"But I'm very particular about my sleeping environment," she said. "Things have to be just right, or I don't sleep at all."

"You don't have any trouble sleeping in my bed," he said.

"That's because your bedroom has solid walls, an adjoining bathroom, 600-count sheets and really nice down pillows. But I did have trouble sleeping that first night. Mostly because we were up so high and I felt the building swaying. Kind of like this boat. And, your clock makes this funny humming sound, so I had to put it inside the drawer." She paused. "Lip balm?"

"All right," Max said. "Lip balm, water, pillow. I'll be right back. If you see any bears, just give me a call."

"There are bears?"

"No," he said. "But if you see any, I want to know." Max grabbed his clothes, then stepped out of the boat to dress on the pier. "You're very high maintenance. Did anyone ever tell you that?"

"Never," she said. "Lip balm, please."

Max walked back to the cabin, laughing softly. This was interesting, he thought to himself. The more comfortable they became with each other, the more he began to discover about her. She was a bit odd, but he liked that about Angela. All her idiosyncrasies were so damn lovable.

He tiptoed into her bedroom and retrieved the tube of lip balm and a pillow, then fetched her a bottle of water. But by the time he got back to the boat, she was asleep. Max stripped off his shorts, then pulled the sleeping bag up around them both.

She sighed softly as she curled her body into his, pressing her face against his shoulder. "Good night, sweetheart," he whispered.

As her breathing slowed, Max silently stroked her back, his eyes closed, his body completely relaxed. Though it always seemed like the most natural thing in the world to make love to Angela, lying beside her like this felt just as good. He could spend his entire life like this, if he chose. He could have her forever.

He'd have to get her to agree, but Max didn't see that as an insurmountable problem. After all, he was a charming guy. And women loved him. But, there was only one woman he wanted and he had to figure out a way to make her need him as much as he needed her.

MAX SAT AT THE BAR, the Tribune sports page spread out in front of him. He scanned the box scores for the Rays, then went though the rest of the scores for the teams in his division.

He and Angela had driven back from Chicago the previous morning and spent the entire day and night in his apartment, curled up in bed watching old movies, eating Szechwan, and reading the Sunday paper.

But when he suggested they spend Tuesday in bed as well, she'd put her foot down. She had to at least make an attempt to go to work on occasion. The more she left for Ceci to do, the further behind they got, she'd argued. So Max had reluctantly kissed her goodbye, pulled on shorts and a T-shirt and gone for a run.

"Hey there!"

Max glanced up to see Dave strolling in through the kitchen door. "Hey. I didn't expect you back until later. It's not even eleven."

"Lauren got us up at the crack of dawn," he said.

She said she wanted to do some gardening. And the kids have swimming lessons this afternoon." Dave tossed his keys on the bar then poured himself a glass of lemonade from the pitcher in the refrigerator. "So, did you have a nice weekend?"

"It was great until my bozo of a brother showed up and ruined it all."

"Sorry. I guess now that you're home, we'll have to schedule our weekends at the cabin. Lauren extends her deepest apologies, as well. Although she was really glad she got a chance to meet Angela. Lauren said you two met in high school. I didn't know Angela went to Evanston. But now that I think of it, I remember a Susan Weatherby. She was really smart."

"We didn't know each other back then."

"Lauren also mentioned that she thought she recognized her from somewhere."

"Susan?"

"No, Angela."

Max looked up from his paper to find Dave watching him with a cautious expression. "From where?"

His older brother winced. "Well, that's the thing. She couldn't remember. So she did an Internet search and…well, she remembered seeing Angela on a morning news show last winter."

Max felt his gut twist as he recognized the look in his brother's eyes. This was not going to be good. Was she a criminal? A bunny boiler? Or even worse—a reporter? "What?"

"Lauren found a video clip. It turns out Angela

Weatherby is writing a book. About dating disasters. I think she might be writing about you."

Max braced his elbow on the edge of the bar, frowning. "Angela? No, she would have told me about that."

"She has a Web site, Max. It's a big collection of dating horror stories. They have files on thousands and thousands of guys, all written by the women they've screwed over. And guess who's on the Web site?"

"Me?"

Dave nodded. "Yeah. You've got a really fat file. Lots of women have a helluva lot to say about you. And none of it is very nice."

"Nah, Lauren must have it wrong. There's probably another Angela Weatherby."

"Look for yourself," Dave said. "You can use the computer in my office. I'm just saying, if you're going to invest time in this girl, maybe you ought to get to know her a little better."

"It's not going to make a difference," Max said. "So she's writing a book."

"And maybe you're just research?"

"Jeez, David, give me a break. We're sleeping together. Don't you think that's a little extreme to be research? She's a nice girl. She wouldn't do that."

"I'm just looking out for you, man. You have to admit that you haven't made a lot of sensible choices when it comes to women. Half of them were flat out crazy, and the other half were only interested in sex."

"And you think Angela fits in one of those two categories?"

"Just go take a look and form your own opinion. I just think you might have a few questions you want answered."

Max stared at his brother for a long moment, then cursed beneath his breath. "All right. I'll go look. But it's not going to make any difference." He shoved away from the bar and stalked back to the office, slamming the door behind him.

Over the next half hour, he looked at every Google link that had to do with Angela Weatherby of Chicago, Illinois. By the time he was finished, Max was forced to admit that he didn't know her at all.

Who the hell was this woman? She seemed to be determined to exact some kind of revenge on any guy who didn't automatically fall in love with the woman he was dating. His own profile was filled with detailed stories of Max Morgan's pathological inability to commit.

Hell, if she'd read his profile, why in the world would she want to date him? If he were a woman, he'd stay as far away from himself as possible. But was he really that bad? He'd never made any promises and then broken them. All the girls he dated knew he wasn't interested in marriage. But they'd all been certain they'd be the one to change him. It's not like he forced them to hop into bed with him. They were perfectly willing partners.

Max leaned back in the desk chair, rubbing his hands over his face. Now that he knew, what was he going to do about it? He could pretend it didn't make a difference, but he knew it did.

How had he missed this? His experience being in the public eye had given him a keen radarlike sense that detected anyone with suspicious motives. When he'd come home to Chicago, he'd let his guard down and shut the radar off. And now, he was left to wonder just who Angela Weatherby really was.

Max pushed away from the desk and walked back out into the bar. "I'll see you later," he muttered as he passed Dave.

"Hey, didn't I tell you? It's weird, huh?"

Max's jaw tensed as he fought the impulse to turn around and curse a blue streak at his brother. Though he ought to appreciate the fraternal loyalty, he didn't like his family interfering in his social life. But wasn't that what he'd come to Chicago for—to be closer to his family? When it came down to it, he'd always trust them first.

When he got out to the street, Max realized he didn't have his car. He'd either have to run back home or run all the way to Wicker Park to talk to Angela. He turned west, toward Angela, and toward the answers he needed.

By the time he reached Angela's office, he was drenched in sweat and even angrier than he was when he'd left the bar. He wiped his face on his T-shirt, then walked inside. A receptionist sat at a desk in the lobby, her gaze fixed on her computer. She turned and smiled and then caught her breath in surprise. "Hello," she said. "You're—"

"Angela Weatherby," Max interrupted. "Can you tell me where her office is?"

"Down that hall and to your right. Last door."

When he found the office, Max drew a deep breath and then opened the door. Though he wasn't sure what he planned to say, he knew he'd come up with something the moment he saw her. Unfortunately, he saw Ceci first. She stood beside a table, a sheaf of papers in her hand, a stunned expression on her face.

"Max. Hi."

"Ceci." He glanced around. "So this is where you two work." The tension had seeped into his voice and Ceci forced a smile as she glanced around nervously.

Ceci's shoulders slumped and she sent him an apologetic smile. "Max, believe me, she never thought anything would happen with you two. She just wanted to interview you. And I think, part of her wanted to see if the feelings she had for you so long ago were finally gone. I talked her into going out that night. If I hadn't, you two would have never met. She wouldn't have gone on her own."

"Why do I feel like I'm only getting half the story? First, she doesn't know me. Then she does. Then she was madly in love with me. And now—I don't know what's going on now."

"Maybe you better talk to her. She just went out to get coffee. She'll be back in a few minutes." Ceci grabbed her purse from a nearby chair. "I'm just going to leave you two alone."

"That would probably be best," he muttered.

She stopped halfway out the door, then turned back. "For what it's worth, I really do think she loves you. She just wasn't prepared to still feel that way. And certainly not after a week. You caught her by surprise."

"Everything seems to be catching me by surprise," Max said.

The door swung closed and Max was left in the silent office. He sat down in one of the desk chairs, bracing his elbows on his knees as he shoved his fingers through his damp hair. He wasn't sure whether to believe Ceci or not. Did Angela love him or was Ceci simply trying to cover for her friend?

A minute later, the door opened again. Angela froze when she saw him, two large paper cups in her left hand. For a moment, her arm wavered and Max jumped up and grabbed the coffees from her, setting them on a nearby desk.

"Tell me something," Max said, his gaze fixed on the coffees.

"Anything," she said in a shaky voice.

He looked at her, his eyes locking on hers. "Are you writing about me in your book?"

"Am I or was I?" she asked. "There's a difference."

Max cursed softly. "We are not going to play word games, Angela. Am I in your book? Yes or no?"

"Yes," she said. "But it's not you. I mean I don't use your name. There's no way anyone would—well, maybe a few people would make the connection, but—no, you're not. Not anymore. I decided to take you out."

"And all that happened between us? Was that just research? Or was all this just some elaborate scheme to meet me?"

"It wasn't research. And it wasn't a scheme." She took a step toward him, then stopped when he held out his hand. "I know this all looks bad," Angela continued, "but it's not. I have never done anything more than love you. It sounds stupid, but I think I knew the moment we met that we belonged together. All those years ago. And then again, in the bar that night. Ceci thinks it's karma and I have no idea if she's right. But I think I've been waiting for you my whole life. Kind of like those penguins."

"And this is the way you get my attention? By trashing my name on the Internet?"

"It wasn't me," Angela explained. "Those women have a right to their opinions. I—I don't happen to share their views, but that doesn't make their feelings any less valid. Max, I didn't expect to feel this way. I just wanted to prove that you were everything they said you were. And that these feelings I had for you were silly and childish. Only you weren't…and my feelings weren't. I didn't know what to do."

"The truth might have been nice."

Angela nodded, a tear sliding down her cheek. "Probably. But after a while, I just didn't want to ruin it. I figured you'd put an end to it sooner or later. I guess this is it."

Max closed his eyes and leaned back in the chair. "You knew how I felt about the press. What you're doing here isn't much different."

"No," Angela said. "It's not. And I can understand how you might think it's an invasion of your privacy. But maybe you need to see a bit of truth in it as well. These women all felt they had a good reason for writing about you. And I think, if you're honest with yourself, you know you didn't treat them well."

"So you think I deserve to have my reputation trashed?"

"No. But I think my opinion of you might be a bit prejudiced. We are sleeping together." Angela took a ragged breath. "I didn't know what to do. Being with you was like a fantasy come true. I couldn't help myself from getting caught up in it."

"That doesn't make me feel any better."

"I'm not going to make excuses," Angela said. "This is what I do for a living. You don't have to like it."

"But you're doing it to me," he said. "What does that say about us?"

"There was no *us* a week ago," Angela said. "And

I'm not sure there'll be an *us* next week. I don't know how this is going to turn out, Max, but if your profile is any evidence, it's not going to turn out well. I'm going to be just another notch on your bedpost."

"How can you be such an optimist and a cynic at the same time?" he asked, shaking his head.

"That's always been my problem. I want the fantasy, but I'm too practical to believe it when I get it." She closed the door and crossed the office. Kneeling down in front of him, she placed her hands on his knees. "I know I've probably messed this up. And I don't know if you can forgive me. But if you can't, I'm all right with that. I had my chance and I blew it. But at least I had my chance. No matter what you say to me, I don't regret it."

Max looked down at her, his anger waning. He wanted to gather her in his arms and kiss her until all the confusion went away, until he was sure of his feelings again. But at the moment, he wasn't certain of anything. He quickly stood, stepping around her, and walked to the door before he could touch her.

"I have to go. I'll talk to you later."

Angela sat down on the floor, then nodded as he closed the door. Max stopped, bracing his hand on the wall as he looked back at office. Every instinct told him to go back inside, to begin again, to forget everything that had happened. This was a woman who had just admitted she loved him and he was ready to throw that all away because of—of what?

He needed time to sort this all out. Time to figure

out exactly where Angela belonged in his life. She'd been a part of his past. Would she be a part of his future, too?

"YOU KNEW THIS MIGHT HAPPEN," Ceci said. "There is no such thing as anonymity in the age of Google. So how did you leave it?"

"He walked out."

"That's it?"

"He said, see you later. But he says that to everyone."

Ceci smiled wanly. "Well, maybe he means it this time. Maybe he just needs time to think this out."

"No. It's definitely over," said Angela, shaking her head. "And that's good. I accomplished what I set out to do. I got to know him. I turned the fantasy into reality. He seduced me and he dumped me. My thesis is proved."

"And that makes you happy?"

"No," Angela said. "But I'm back to where I was before we met. Only now, I won't have to compare every guy I meet to Max Morgan. He will not be the standard by which every other man in my life is judged."

Ceci leaned up against the edge of Angela's desk. "You seem to be handling this very well."

She swallowed back her tears and tried to put on a brave face. "What's there to handle? We were together a week. For Max Morgan, that's pretty good." A tear trickled down her cheek and then, a sob slipped out.

Angela couldn't seem to stop herself. Her composure was shattered.

Ceci gathered her in her arms. "Oh, sweetie, I'm sorry."

"You should be," Angela replied, forcing a laugh. "I told you you'd have to pick up the pieces." She wiped her damp cheeks with her fingers. "I tried not to fall in love with him but it was so difficult. He is a devil. He tempted me and I just…cracked." Angela drew a ragged breath. "But I had fun. The sex was great. And I got to do some interesting things."

A soft knock sounded on the office door and a few moments later, Will stepped inside. Ceci turned, her arms still around Angela. "Hi. You're early."

"Yeah. I thought you'd be too excited to wait."

Angela glanced back and forth between them. "Excited about what?"

Ceci shook her head, stepping away to grab her purse. "Now's not a good time," she said. "We'll tell you later."

"Tell me what? I'm fine, really."

"She just broke up with Max," Ceci explained. "I really don't think—"

Angela cursed softly. "What?"

Ceci bit her bottom lip. "Will and I are engaged. He proposed last night and I said yes."

Angela felt the tears start again, only these were tears of happiness. "Oh, Ceci, that's wonderful. So you had your moment?"

"The mustard stain at the baseball game. That was it."

Angela hugged Will. "You'll be so happy. I know you will. You picked the best girl."

Ceci wrapped her arms around Will's waist and they all hugged each other. "He's my guy! Besides, if I didn't marry him, who would?"

"I think it's perfect," Angela said through her tears.

"Stop crying or I'm going to start. Why don't we all go out for a glass of wine?"

Angela drew a calming breath. "You two go. I'll be fine. I have some work to do on the book." She gave them a little wave as they walked out. Then, pressing her lips together, she fought back another surge of tears. She was happy for them, really she was. But she couldn't help but wonder if she'd ever find a guy who loved her as much as Will loved Ceci.

She sat down at her desk, cupping her chin in her palm as she scrolled through the site. She clicked to the main menu and then typed in a search for Max's name. His profile came up, along with a series of photos that the women had posted.

As she looked at each one, Angela was struck by how none of the photos resembled the man she knew. For all she could tell, she was looking at a complete stranger. Max's smile was warmer, and his eyes darker, and the dimple in his cheek deeper.

She knew every post in his profile by heart but as she read through them again, it was clear that they'd never known the real Max Morgan. Angela closed her eyes and cursed softly. Or maybe she was the one who'd never known him.

When she'd finally regained her composure, Angela opened the site maintenance program and found the tab to delete a profile. Then she clicked over to Max's. She and Ceci had always been adamant about their own neutrality in editing the site. Profiles were meant to inform, not to slander. It was a fine line to walk, but Angela had been proud of the job they'd done so far.

Deleting a profile had never been an option. If one of the men got married, the profile was tagged, but not deleted. She drew a deep breath, the pointer hovering over the delete button. It was the least she could do for him. And if someone complained, they could always write it off as a technical glitch.

Drawing a deep breath, Angela clicked and Max Morgan disappeared from SmoothOperators.com. She felt as if an unbearable weight had been lifted. The deception, though not forgotten, was at least undone. She pulled up the manuscript for her book and found Chapter Five. Unfortunately, this wasn't quite as easy to delete.

It was just one chapter. Would he even recognize himself in her words? There were eleven other archetypes in the book. No, she wouldn't delete it. She'd simply change the title of the chapter. "The Sexy Sinner," she murmured. "The Sexy Scoundrel." Angela nodded. That would work.

When she'd saved her change, Angela turned off her computer and grabbed her bag. The past week had been a whirlwind of emotion. It was time to get her life back on track. Tuesday night was laundry night. She'd have time to give herself a pedicure, catch up on all her reading, and take a long hot bath.

There was a time she'd actually enjoyed her single life. She could find that happiness again. Angela walked to the door, but as she opened it, the office phone rang. She hesitated, desperate to leave business behind. But then she walked back inside.

"Hello, this is Angela."

"Angela! Kelly Caulfield at Daybreak Chicago. How are you?"

"Hello. I'm fine. How are you?"

"Well, we have an opening in our schedule for Thursday morning. One of our guests cancelled. And since you were so great when you were on with us in January, I was hoping you might come back and do another segment."

"Thursday morning?"

"Yes. I know it's short notice, but I'm really desperate. This would be a huge favor and I promise that we'll have you on again to plug your book when it comes out. In fact, you can pick the date."

"I don't know, I—"

"Please," Kelly said. "Did I mention we're desperate?"

"Yes. All right. What time do I need to be there?"

"We're going to give you a later spot, so if you arrive by 7:15, we'll be fine. Thank you so much! Our graphic guy is going to pull some shots from the Web site. If you have a cover for the book and a solid release date, we can mention that, too."

"I do have a cover," Angela said. "But I'm really not sure of the release date."

"Bring it along and we'll get it up anyway. Thank you again. I'll see you Thursday morning."

Angela hung up the phone. This was beyond strange. It was as if her life was rewinding, back to a time when everything seemed to be moving along quite nicely. But could she really go back after what she'd experienced in the last week?

She walked out into the warm evening, heading toward her flat. She'd spend the night alone. It felt strange to have no plans, nothing to look forward to. Just her empty bed and a quiet house.

On her way home, she stopped at the grocery store and picked up dinner, a salad, soup and some freshly baked bread. As she passed the dessert case, she picked up a small strawberry cheesecake.

At times like this, when her life looked a little bleak, eating an entire cheesecake was the only prescription for happiness. And it was just a small cheesecake.

Her flat was silent and cool as she stepped inside. The place was a bit messy. Over the past week, she'd run in and out, to dress, to shower, to get ready for fun with Max. She kicked her sandals off and walked into the kitchen, setting the bags on the granite countertop.

She picked up her phone, then set it down before listening to her voice mail signal. He wasn't going to call. And waiting for him was only going to drive her crazy. But her curiosity got the better of her and she picked up and dialed. "One message," she murmured, listening to the number. It was Max's home number and he'd left the message early that morning. She held her breath, then replayed the message.

"Hi. It's me. You just left for work and I'm lying here in my bed wondering what we're going to do tonight. I think you should put on your prettiest dress and I'll take you out for dinner. I have something I need to talk to you about. Don't worry. Nothing bad. I'll see you later. Love you."

"Love me," she muttered. "Not anymore."

She hung up the phone, then retrieved the bottle of wine from the fridge and yanked out the cork. Not bothering with a glass, Angela took a drink of the Chardonnay, straight from the bottle. There was a half bottle left. She'd have to be careful. The last thing she wanted to do was drink too much and start drunk dialing.

Setting the wine down, Angela grabbed the bag with the cheesecake in it. She retrieved a fork and dug in, then carried the box with her to her bedroom. When she'd settled herself in the center of the bed, she flipped on the television and began to devour the cheesecake. "So this is my life," she murmured. "Empty calories and reality television."

There was one bright spot. It could only get better from here.

8

THE ACHE IN HIS HEAD throbbed along with his pulse, an incessant rhythm that kept him from falling back asleep. Max rolled over in bed and pulled the pillow over his head, blocking out the early morning rays of the sun. He peeked at the bedside clock then groaned. Four hours of sleep was usually not enough for him, especially if it came after a night of too many beers.

He threw his arm out on the opposite side of the bed, just to make sure there was no one else in the room with him. He'd been almost drunk enough to bring a woman home. But not quite. In truth, he probably would have passed out before he drank enough to put Angela out of his mind for good.

He'd spent the last couple days trying desperately to forget her. When beer didn't do the trick, he ran, miles and miles, pushing his body until he couldn't run any longer. Running, drinking, sleeping and then doing it all over again. Anything to wear his body out so his mind wouldn't have the energy to remember how good he'd had it.

Reaching out again, he searched the bed for the remote control, then flipped on the television, anxious for the drone of the morning news to put him back to sleep. Max closed his eyes and drew a deep breath.

But just as he was drifting back into unconsciousness, he heard her voice, soft, sweet, a sound he'd come to crave over the last few days. Cursing softly, he threw aside the pillow and sat up. A groan rumbled in his chest as his head threatened to explode with the pain. But her voice was still there.

Max stared at the television, giving his eyes a moment to focus. When they did, he realized Angela really was there, on television, talking about her Web site. He sat numbly, listening to her voice but not bothering to comprehend the words she was saying.

She looked tired, he thought to himself. But she was still beautiful, her honey-blond hair falling around her shoulders, her lush lips forming each word. Max crawled to the end of the bed to get a better look. He stared at her eyes, fascinated by the color. High definition plasma televisions were a wonderful invention, he mused.

Before long, the hostess wrapped up the interview and Angela was gone. An odd sense of loss settled in his gut. Was that the last time he'd ever see her? Max had fought with himself over the past few days, wanting to call her, thinking that they might be able to work it out, and then knowing that he'd be heading back to Florida in a few weeks to rejoin the team.

What was the use? Long distance relationships never worked. They'd be apart at least until the end of the regular season. And if the team made it into the playoffs, until late October.

After that, he was in charge. Free agency was a complicated affair, but Max had an ace to play. He was willing to walk away from the game if he didn't get what he wanted. If he was going to play another year, Max wanted to finish his career in Chicago. If he could get the Rays to trade him or release him, he'd be able to negotiate a deal to make the move. Money didn't make a difference anymore, so chances were, he could make it work.

But what was the use coming back to Chicago if he wasn't going to be with Angela. Sure, he wanted to be near his family, but Angela was the reason he was considering a move north. But right now, they weren't even talking to each other.

His phone rang beside the bed and Max frowned. Only one person called him this early in the morning—his mother. No doubt she wanted to firm up plans for Saturday's barbecue. He'd decided to attend, hoping some time with the family would take his mind off Angela. And maybe, just maybe, she might decide to come.

"Hi, Mom," he said. "What's up?"

"She was just on the news. Did you catch it? Channel Seven."

"Actually, I did catch it."

"She's lovely, isn't she? I told you. Now why wouldn't you want to go out with a woman like that?"

"I'm coming on Saturday," he said.

"These models and actresses. They just have their minds on other things. They don't—"

"Mom, I said I'd be there."

"Really?" Max heard her cover the phone with her hand and shout to his father. "Max is coming to the barbecue!"

"What time do you want me to come around?" he asked.

"Noon. She's coming at one. And wear something nice. Not those raggedy shorts you always have on."

"We've already discussed the wardrobe, Mom." He paused, fighting back an impulse. In the end, though, Max decided that if his mother was going to run his social life anyway, he might as well get something out of the deal. "Make sure you call this girl and let her know that I'm anxious to meet her. Tell her I'm really looking forward to it."

"Really?"

"Of course. If she's as great as you say she is, then I'm sure I'll like her. But I'm not going to come if she doesn't come. Tell her that."

"All right," Maggie Morgan said. "I'll see you Saturday."

She hung up and Max tossed the cordless phone onto the bed. Then he flopped down and covered his face with the pillow again. What was the use in trying to stay away? He needed to see Angela again.

The anger he'd felt a few days ago had dissolved with time and now, he was left with the realization that what had happened hadn't changed his feelings for her. He really liked Angela. He probably even loved her. Not probably, he did love her. And Max had never felt that way about a woman before.

He crawled out of bed and grabbed a pair of running shorts from the pile of clean clothes on a nearby chair, then tugged on a T-shirt. His shoes were next to the door and once he got them on, Max headed out, jogging slowly to warm-up, then began to run in earnest.

It was like some invisible force was drawing him toward her. He just wanted to make sure she was all right. Max wasn't sure what he planned to do once he got to her neighborhood, but he felt an overwhelming need to see her again.

He stopped in for a latte and a Danish at the Starbucks closest to her place, then walked to her flat carrying her breakfast in a bag. As he waited on her stoop, Max wasn't sure he was ready to talk to her. What was he supposed to say? He needed a plan, something to offer her, a way that they could move forward.

Maybe it would have been better to have just waited until Saturday. Max left the coffee and Danish on the step and started down the block. But before he turned the corner, he glanced back. He saw her, walking toward her flat, dressed in the clothes she'd worn on television.

Max hid behind a nearby tree, watching her. "Now who's the stalker?" he muttered.

Angela stopped short when she saw the coffee and the paper bag with the Danish. She looked up and down the street, then slowly picked it up. Max smiled to himself. She had to know where it had come from. He wondered what was going through her mind.

A few moments later, she took one last look around, then disappeared inside. Max decided to wait and see her when she came out again. If he ran around the block, he'd be able to run into her, as if it were an accidental meeting. They could chat, he could read her mood and maybe figure out where he stood.

But his wait was interrupted when he heard the piercing sound of a police siren. The noise startled him and he spun around to see a patrol car parked right behind him. The policeman rolled down his window and leaned out.

"You wanna tell me what—" He paused. "Hey, you're Max Morgan, aren't you?"

Max nodded. "Yeah, I am."

"What are you doing here?"

"Just standing," he said. Max pointed to his leg. "Cramp."

"Oh, yeah? You eat bananas? I find that if I eat a banana a day, I don't have trouble with leg cramps. I think it's the potassium."

"Thanks for the advice," Max said.

"No problem." He nodded. "I'm gonna have to tell you to move along, though. We had a call from one of the neighbors. She's worried you might be casing her place for a burglary. These older folks get a little nervous when they see strangers on the street."

"No problem," Max said.

The policeman nodded. "A lot of burglars pose as runners. If they get caught, they can escape pretty quick." The guy chuckled. "But, hey, I don't think you'd need to burgle in order to make money. You've got a nice contract down there in Florida, don't you?"

"Actually, I'm a free agent after this season."

"Aw, man, you've gotta come back and play for the Sox. They could use a hitter like you." The radio on his shoulder crackled. He pushed a button and listened to the call. "Gotta go. Fender bender on North. Take care now."

Max chuckled to himself as he took one last look down the street. After another ten minutes, Angela still hadn't emerged. Maybe she'd gone back to bed, Max thought. He stretched out his calf muscle, then jogged across the street and headed back toward the lake.

"I'll see you soon, Angela," he murmured.

THE MORGANS LIVED IN a beautiful old house near Ingleside Park in Evanston. As Angela searched for a place to park on the street, she drove past a familiar black BMW. "Oh dear. What am I doing here?" She drew a deep breath. She'd been invited. If she didn't go, she'd never hear the end of it from her mother.

If she did go, then she'd definitely be seeing Max again. Just once more, just enough time to set things straight. Angela was certain she could finally put their relationship in perspective. There were no hard feelings, at least on her part, and she hoped he felt the same way.

After she parked, Angela twisted the rearview mirror toward her and examined her hair and make-up. This would be his last memory of her and she wanted it to be a good one. Not that he'd give her a second thought once he found a new woman to occupy his time. But someday, he might look back on what they shared and realize it had been good—for a little while, at least.

Angela hopped out of her car and hurried down the sidewalk toward the house. The barbecue had started at one, but she'd spent some time driving around her hometown in an attempt to work up her courage. She'd turned the car south more than once, but in the end, she'd decided she wanted to end this with no regrets. She wouldn't spend another fourteen years thinking about what might have been if she'd only attended the Morgan barbecue.

The front door was open and she recognized the two girls standing behind the screen. Angela smiled and waved at Brit and Beth. "Hello there."

"Angela!" they shouted as they shoved open the door and stumbled outside. They met her in the middle of the walk, each grabbing a hand and pulling her toward the house. "You're here," Brit said. "Why didn't you come with Uncle Max?"

"Can we play a game?" Beth asked. "Grammy has Chutes and Ladders. Have you ever played Apples to Apples? Grammy has that game, too. Do you want to play that?"

They ushered her into the spacious foyer and then through a beautiful living room. When they reached a great room at the back of the house, she could see the party through the wall of windows that overlooked the backyard. "We brought our dog," Brittany said. "We don't take him to the cabin because he throws up in the car on long trips. His name is Elwood."

"Girls, take the guests to the backyard, please. That's your job."

Angela held her breath at the sound of his voice and when Max came around the corner from the kitchen, their eyes met. A long silence grew between them and the little girls looked back and forth, their expressions curious.

"It's Angela," Beth said. "Say hello to her, Uncle Max."

"Right," Max said, forcing a smile. "Hello. I wasn't sure you'd be coming."

"Duh," Brittany said, rolling her eyes. "She's your girlfriend. Why wouldn't she come?"

"Maybe she had a tummy ache," Bethany said. "I had a tummy ache and I couldn't go to day camp yesterday."

"Girls, head back to the door. I'll show Angela out to the backyard." Max shooed them off, then turned to Angela. His gaze searched her face and Angela felt a flush warm her cheeks. "I'm glad you came," he murmured.

"I thought we needed to see each other once more," she said. "Just to...settle things."

Max glanced over his shoulder at the crowd in the backyard. Then he grabbed her hand and pulled her along after him. But instead of going outside, he took her up a rear stairway that led from the kitchen to the second floor. At the end of the hall, they stepped inside a bedroom and he closed the door behind them both.

Angela looked around at the shelves of baseball trophies that lined the walls. This was his room. She walked over to the dresser and studied the items displayed on the top. "This looks a lot different than your condo," she said. Angela pointed to the trophies. "You should move these down there. They'd impress the girls you bring home."

"Maybe," he said. "Would they have impressed you?"

She turned and smiled at him. "Nothing impresses me."

"That's right," he said. "I forgot."

Angela sat down on the edge of the bed and looked up at him. He looked so handsome in a blue oxford shirt and khakis. She'd become so accustomed to seeing him in various states of undress that she'd never appreciated how well he wore clothes. "I wanted to tell you I'm sorry I wasn't completely honest with you from the start. I guess I never thought we'd even speak to each other, much less spend any time together. And then, things started happening so fast, there never seemed to be the right moment."

He sat down beside her. "I may have overreacted," Max said. "The truth is, until you came along, I didn't much think about the impression I was leaving with the women I knew. I didn't really care."

"And now you do?"

Max took her hand and wove his fingers through hers. "I care about what you think," he said. "I don't want you to have any regrets."

"I don't," Angela said.

He brought her hand to his lips and kissed the back of her wrist, his warm mouth lingering on her skin. Angela's heart fluttered and a tiny sigh slipped from her throat. The sensation was so familiar. Her mind flashed back to a time when his lips had traveled all over her naked body.

How difficult would it be to just pull him down on the bed and kiss him? How would he react? Angela didn't have to guess. The answer was in his touch, in the gentle caress of his fingers on her wrist. He still wanted her as much as she wanted him. "How is your shoulder?" she asked.

"Better."

"So, you'll be going back to Florida soon?"

He nodded. "Actually, I'm flying back tomorrow." He paused. "But I don't have to. I mean, I could fly back—"

"I'm glad," she said, pasting a bright smile on her face.

"That I'm leaving?"

Angela shook her head. "No, that your shoulder has healed."

Without warning, Max took her face in his hands and kissed her. Angela drew back, startled, staring up into his gaze without blinking. But then, he tried again and she felt her defenses crumble. Why go on fooling herself? She wanted to kiss him. She wanted to rip off all her clothes and make love to him on his baseball bedspread.

He must have had the same thought because as the kiss spun out, he gently drew her down onto the bed. It amazed her how perfectly they read each other's desires. Her fingers fumbled with the buttons on his shirt and when she'd managed to undo three or four, Angela smoothed her hand over his muscled chest.

"I've missed you," he murmured, furrowing

his fingers through her hair and pulling her into a deeper kiss.

"You better find a way to stop that," she said. He frowned, meeting her gaze. "You're going back to Florida tomorrow."

"If you ask me to stay, I will." He kissed her again, his passion rising. "Ask me."

It was just one word. "Stay." And her entire life would change. But it wasn't that simple. He had a job in Florida, a life, and a career. And everything she'd built for herself was here in Chicago. But for a chance at love—at real, forever love—wouldn't she give it all up?

"I can't," she said. "You have to go back."

"You could come with me?"

Angela shook her head. "We've known each other for…well, it hasn't been two weeks yet."

"It doesn't make a difference," Max said.

"Yes, it does," Angela said. "We're in that stage when all our flaws are hidden and we think we're perfect for each other."

"You have no flaws," he said, finding a spot just below her ear to kiss.

Angela gently pushed him away. For once in her life, she wasn't going to give in to her fantasies. She was going to do the right thing, the practical thing. "You need to go back, Max. And then, when the season is over, we can see how we feel."

"I already know how I'll feel," Max said. "I need you."

She opened her mouth, then paused before speaking. "Do you need me? Or do you just need a woman? Maybe you need to find out for sure."

An astonished look crossed his face and he regarded her warily. "That's a lovely offer, but I don't think I'll be taking advantage of that. Now that I've decided which woman I want, another one won't do." He reached out and cupped her face in his hand. "I've fallen in love with you, Angela. There won't be any other women in my life from now on."

Angela felt emotion clog her throat. How long had she waited to hear those words? Every dream she'd had about him had always ended in a sweet confession of his feelings for her. But now, she couldn't quite bring herself to believe him.

Ceci was right. The Web site had changed her. She couldn't look at love without a healthy dose of cynicism. She wanted to believe it could exist, but Angela needed proof. If he went back to his life and then returned, she'd know for sure. "I think you should go," she said.

"We'll both go."

She shook her head, but Max kissed her again. "I was about to leave anyway. I came to meet this girl and she didn't show up. Besides, I only have a day left in Chicago. I don't want to spend it with my parents and their friends. I want to spend it with you."

They walked to the door. "I should at least go in and say hello to my parents," Angela said.

He took her hand and led her to the stairs in the

front of the house. "If we sneak out, no one will even know where we've gone."

"Where are we going?" Angela asked.

"Somewhere we can be alone."

The girls were waiting at the front door. Max ruffled their hair. "Go tell Grammy that I really like the girl she found for me and I'm taking her home with me."

The two girls giggled and ran off as Max pulled Angela out the front door. Every shred of common sense had fled. Angela knew she shouldn't jump into bed with him, but that's all she really wanted—to feel his naked body next to hers. To lose herself in the delicious sensations of their lovemaking. She'd survived it all before. One last time couldn't hurt her.

"I'll meet you at your place," she said.

MAX STARED OUT AT THE water of the Gulf, watching a trio of pelicans float lazily on the surface. He ran his hands through his hair, waiting for that sense of calm to settle in. That's what he loved about his house in Florida. He could just open the door and listen to the waves on the shore, Everything was perfect.

But since he'd returned, that calm had been disrupted by nearly constant thoughts of Angela. They'd spent one last day and night together and then she was gone, sneaking out of his bed in the predawn hours.

In truth, Max had been glad there wouldn't be any

dramatic good-byes. It would be as if she'd just gone to work while he slept late. A day would pass, he'd call her and they'd pretend they weren't miles apart. The months would pass and the season would end and they'd be together again.

They'd talked on the phone a few times, but once again, they never seemed to have the same connection. She sounded distant and he fumbled for things to talk about. He needed to be able to reach out and touch her, to let his hands and his lips say the things he couldn't put into words.

The team had a three-game series in Chicago next month. Even though he was still on the disabled list, the series would give him a good excuse to fly back to Chicago for the weekend and see her.

Max sighed. He shouldn't need an excuse, but there was so much unsettled between them. It was clear that Angela was not hopeful about their future. Already, she'd begun preparing for the worst, assuming that everything would fall apart once they were apart. Somewhere along the line, the fantasy had disappeared and she'd begun to see the reality in front of her.

Max's doorbell buzzed and he glanced at the clock on the mantel. He walked to the front door, his footsteps silent on the cool tile. His agent, Bruce Carmichael, was standing on the other side, dressed in a ridiculous Hawaiian shirt and cargo shorts. "You look hot," Max said, stepping aside to let him in. "And I don't mean that in a sexual way."

"I love you, too, Max, but I hate where you live. You know, it's exactly the same temperature here as it is in L.A. And yet this feels so much more like hell."

"It's the humidity," Max said walking back into the airy living room. "Sit. Do you want something to drink?"

"Ice water. Lots of ice," he said.

In the kitchen, Max filled a huge glass at the sink and then grabbed a beer for himself before returning to the living room. He sat down and took a long swallow of his beer.

"What's up?" Bruce said. "Why did you make me fly all the way out here?"

"I've got some plans and I need you to make them happen," he said.

"Plans? What kind of plans?"

"I want to play in Chicago next season."

"What? No, I don't think that's going to happen. You're a marquee player and the Rays—"

"I'm a marquee player with a bad shoulder," Max reminded him. "I might not come back."

"Still, if they trade you, they're going to expect a draft pick and some major money. There isn't a team out there who'll bite unless you finish the season strong."

"But if I tell them I'm going to retire if they don't trade me, they might think differently."

Bruce leaned forward, concern etched deeply into his expression. "You're thinking about retiring?"

"It's an option. I might not have a choice if the shoulder doesn't come back. This can work," Max said. "We have the advantage. We just have to play it right."

"If you recover completely, you could play another five or six years. I thought you liked playing for the Rays."

"I do. They're a great team. But I have other reasons for wanting to play for Chicago. You do what it takes to get me there, all right?"

"You have to at least consider other offers," Bruce said. "If the Rays give you the best offer, then you have to take it."

"No, I don't. I'd retire. I'm looking at the end of my career, Bruce. And for once, I want to make a decision that doesn't involve money. I want to make a decision because my heart tells me it's right."

Bruce frowned. "Is this about a girl?"

"No!" Max replied. "Well, yeah, I guess it is. But what's wrong with that? I've made enough money to keep both of us comfortable for the rest of our lives. I've invested well. Now, I want to do something that would make me happy."

Bruce sighed. "I suppose I can put out some feelers and see what they'd be willing to do," he said. "But you're tying my hands. I'm supposed to get you the best deal and this won't be it."

"Do your magic. If I'm playing next year, I want to play in Chicago." Max got to his feet. "Now that we have the rest of my life settled, do you want to do some fishing? I haven't had the boat out in months. And it's much cooler on the water."

Bruce nodded. "Sure. What are we going to fish for?"

"We'll figure that out when we get there," Max said with a shrug.

His agent chuckled. "What is wrong with you? Where is the Max Morgan I know and love? I'm not used to seeing you so…relaxed."

"I'm getting ready to live the rest of my life," Max said. "I've got new priorities." He pulled the door open and Bruce walked through. "I'm thinking I might even get married. Maybe start a family."

"I don't know," Bruce said. "With this kind of attitude, how are you ever going to find someone to marry? You're not going to have a job and you'll be hanging around the house all day. Once you stop working out, you're going to put on some weight. And if you stop with the women, you're going to lose all your charm. Who would marry that?"

"I have someone in mind," Max said. "I just need some time to convince her. But I can't do that if I'm living in Florida."

"What are you going to do with this house?"

"I don't know. Maybe keep it as a vacation home. I need to have somewhere to escape to during those Chicago winters. And this place has a pool with a very high privacy fence."

Bruce frowned. "What the hell does that have to do with anything?"

"Nothing," Max said with a chuckle. At least nothing he wanted to discuss with his agent. His mind wandered back to the night he and Angela had spent skinny-dipping in the lake. Really, it didn't matter where they lived.

He could be happy in her little one-bedroom flat in Wicker Park. As long as she crawled into bed with him at night and woke up in his arms in the morning, Max would be content. "One more thing. I need you to keep this quiet," Max said. "No press speculation, no interviews about why I'm thinking of moving. When it's done, we can talk, but not until then."

"I don't know. Everyone is already wondering what's going to happen with you. It'll be difficult to keep the press out of it."

Max chuckled, clapping Bruce on the shoulder. His life was falling into place. He was only missing one thing—the girl. "I know you can handle it. That's why I pay you the big bucks, right?"

2

"WHAT IS THIS?" Ceci stared at the manila envelope Angela was holding out to her across the table.

They'd had a leisurely lunch, sitting at an outdoor café, but Angela had been anxious to get back to business. "It's an early wedding present," she said with a smile.

Ceci laughed, then rolled her eyes. "Will and I are not getting married tomorrow. We haven't even set a date yet. Or agreed on a concept. Will wants to elope to Vegas. And I'm beginning to think I look really fat in white, so I'm pushing for the beach in September. Kind of a hippie-retro wedding."

"Open it," Angela said.

Ceci pulled the legal papers out and frowned. "Are we being sued?"

"I'm turning the Web site over to you," Angela said. "It's all yours."

"What?"

"You can have it all, Ceci. I can't do this anymore.

I want to believe I can fall in love. I did fall in love for a little while. But this Web site is just a reminder of how wrong I was."

"That doesn't mean you have to give up everything we've worked for." Ceci stared at the papers in disbelief.

"I need to move on," Angela said. "I have a couple of job prospects. The neighborhood business association is looking for a director and I applied for the job. I've also got a freelance offer to write a relationship column for a women's magazine."

"But you could do those things and still work here. I can't do this on my own, Angie. I don't want to. I love coming to work with you. It's fun. Who am I going to walk with in the morning? Who am I going to have coffee with? And all our lunches and late dinners."

"Whom," Angela said.

"Stop! I'm serious."

"None of that will change," Angela said. "I'm not going anywhere. If I work for the neighborhood association, their office is in our building, just up the stairs."

"You're thinking about him, aren't you," Ceci said. "You're thinking you might leave Chicago and move to Florida. That's it, isn't it? We can't have coffee if you're in Florida!"

Angela took a quick sip of her lemonade. "I'm not going to Florida. Max and I aren't going to work this out. He'll soon forget all about me. I'm here to stay and I'll always be your best friend."

"What about the book?"

"It was a bad idea. I was completely wrong about my thesis, but my editor says it will still sell. So, I'm putting your name on the cover."

"Mine?"

"You were my coauthor and you've helped me with a lot of the research. You can do all the press for it and promote the site. It'll be fun. Besides, you like doing that stuff much more than I do."

"This is about Max, isn't it," Ceci said. "Are you doing this because you still love him?"

"No, I'm doing this because he might still love me," Angela said. "If he does and he comes back, then I don't want anything to get between us."

"Are you sure about this?" Ceci asked.

"I am. It's time to be more optimistic, Ceci. You've always been optimistic about love and look where you are. You're about to marry Will and start a wonderful new life."

Ceci stared down at the papers, a dejected look on her face. "I wasn't going to mention this, but we had a call last month from someone who wanted to buy the site. He wasn't offering much and I figured you wouldn't want to sell, but it would be enough to start up a new business for both of us. We work so well together. Between the two of us, we could come up with a really great idea."

"We'll talk about it," Angela said. "For now, I'm going to keep my options open."

Ceci jumped up and leaned over the table, throwing her arms around Angela and giving her a fierce hug. "I hope things turn out with Max. I really like him."

"And if they don't turn out, then there will be another guy," Angela said. "Optimism. I'm thinking positively. There will be another guy. I'm sure of it. Because for every woman, there is the perfect man waiting for her…somewhere. I just have to find him."

They were still hugging each other when Will walked up to the table. He grinned. "This is the second time I've caught you two in a passionate embrace. Should I be worried?"

Angela laughed. "You caught us. If you're going to marry Ceci, you get me in the deal. We're best friends and I'm not going anywhere. Isn't that every man's fantasy?"

"I can live with that," Will teased. "Although we're going to need a bigger bed."

"Stop," Ceci said. "I'm not sharing my husband with anyone, not even my best friend. How did you know we were here?"

"It's a nice day, you love the chicken salad at the place, and I saw you when I drove by," Will said.

"Sit," Angela said.

"I don't have time. I have to get back to work, but I came here to tell Angela something. Something big.

Really big." He lowered his voice. "This is a secret. Well, not really a secret, since I heard it on the radio, but more like a rumor. Max Morgan may be coming back to Chicago to play for the Sox."

Angela's jaw dropped and she stared at Will, not certain she heard him right. "He can just leave his team and come here?"

"No, there are all sorts of restrictions. He's a free agent at the end of this season. And because of his value to the team, they might not want to let him go. But, if the Rays release him or trade him because of his injury, he could end up back here in Chicago."

Ceci clapped her hands. "He needs to come here. It would be perfect. Like destiny."

"Karma," Angela said. She wasn't sure what to do with the news. In her heart, she wanted to believe she was the reason for his move back to Chicago. But they hadn't really talked about a future together and Max wouldn't make a move like that unless he was sure, would he?

Maybe Max had mastered what Angela still struggled with—optimism. Maybe he was certain they'd be able to work things out once he was back in Chicago. "I should call him," Angela murmured. "I'm going to go home and think about this. It's a lot to take in." She smiled. "Are you sure you heard right, Will?"

Will nodded. "Oh, and you might want to try him on his cell phone because the guy on the radio mentioned that Max is in town and was seen having dinner with a couple Sox players last night."

Angela's heart fell. He was in town and he hadn't bothered to call. If he was doing this for her, wouldn't he have contacted her the moment his plane landed? Wouldn't he have rushed over and dragged her off to the bedroom before doing anything else?

"I'll see you two later." She rubbed her forehead. "Too many things to think about."

Angela walked outside and started in the direction of her flat. But at the last minute, she stepped out to the curb and hailed a passing cab. She gave the cabbie Max's address, then sat back and stared out the window as they made their way east toward the lake.

If he really was thinking about moving back, then Angela needed to know why. He couldn't expect her to start things up again simply because he was living in the same city. There was more than just location keeping them apart.

Or was there? She closed her eyes and drew a deep breath, wrinkling her nose at the smell of air freshener in the cab. She still loved him. Even though she'd tried to convince herself otherwise, the feelings were still there, as strong as ever. Only now, that love was based on an actual relationship and not just a silly fantasy. The Max Morgan she'd dreamed about for years had turned into a man who just might want to spend the rest of his life with her.

Her hands clutched the edge of her seat and she

wiggled her foot nervously. She ought to think about what she was going to say to him. But the only plan she could come up with was to throw herself into his arms and kiss him. After that, it didn't really matter what they said. Kissing always seemed to do the trick with Max.

When she reached his building, Angela paid the cabbie and hurried inside. The doorman was standing behind his desk. He recognized her immediately. "Hello, Miss Weatherby. Is Mr. Morgan with you?"

"No," Angela said. "Actually, I'm supposed to meet him. Do you think I might go upstairs and wait? I'm dying of thirst and I need something cool to drink."

He nodded. "Mr. Morgan left a key with me. He said if you ever needed to get in, I should just give it to you."

"He did? When did he do that?"

"Right after the first time you were here," the doorman said. He handed her a fob with the key dangling from it. "Here you go. You can leave it with me when you go back out."

Angela rode the elevator up and when she got to Max's door, she knocked. Though the doorman implied that Max was out, he could have missed him. After a minute, she put the key in the lock and stepped inside.

It had been over a month since she'd been in his apartment. Angela drew another deep breath and smiled. The place smelled like Max—a wonderful mix of his favorite cologne, leather furniture and the vanilla candles he had scattered on the dining room table.

She dropped her bag on the chair nearest the door and wandered inside. When she got to the bedroom, Angela flopped face down into the rumpled sheets, pulling a pillow under her nose. Strangely enough, the pillow smelled like her shampoo and not Max's cologne.

She stretched out, kicking her sandals off. It felt so good to be back in his bed again. Her eyes fluttered shut. Though she didn't think she'd fallen asleep, Angela had a sense that time had passed when she opened her eyes again. She rolled over and found Max sitting in the chair at the end of the bed, his legs stretched out in front of him, his gaze fixed on her.

"Was I asleep?" she asked, sitting up and smoothing her hand through her mussed hair.

He nodded.

"How long?"

Max smiled. "I've been here for about fifteen minutes. You were asleep when I got here." He stood up and walked across the room, then sat down beside her and smoothed his hand over her bare arm. "What are you doing here, Angela?"

"I came to talk to you."

"How did you know I'd be here?"

"Will said you were in town. I figured you'd have to come home sooner or later. He said you were here to talk about playing in Chicago. Is that true?"

"Unnamed sources," Max said. "Boy, it didn't take the press long. Although, eating lunch with a couple of the players probably wasn't such a great idea."

Angela reached out and rubbed his chest through the crisp fabric of his shirt. It seemed so natural to touch him. She didn't even have to consider how he'd react. "How's the shoulder?"

He shrugged. "It's all right. I've been practicing with the team. I might be able to start playing next month. Then we'll see how it goes."

"Good," she said. "I'm glad everything is turning out all right."

"Almost everything," he said. Max leaned forward and dropped a gentle kiss on her lips. "I think about you all the time, Angela. I think about how good we are together. And how I just want to go back to where things got messed up and figure out how to fix it all. I want you in my life and I'm willing to do whatever it takes to make that happen. If Chicago doesn't make an offer, then I'm going to retire. I'll come back here when my contract runs out and we'll start all over again. Only this time, we won't make any mistakes."

Angela stared into his eyes. The truth was there, so brilliant and clear. "I'm the one who made the mistakes. I didn't believe in what I felt. I couldn't trust my feelings." She reached out and smoothed her hand against his cheek. How many times had she touched him like this and taken it for granted. She'd never do that again. "I'm giving up the Web site. And the book. I don't believe in my thesis anymore."

"What was your thesis?"

"That most men are creeps and they'll take advantage of women if given the opportunity. I believe that men never change and women who think they can change them are just deluded fools. That, for some people, there is no happily ever after."

"So, what do you think about us?" he asked. "Is there reason to be hopeful?"

"Maybe," Angela said. "It would help if you'd kiss me again."

He leaned forward and touched his lips to hers. But what started as a simple contact dissolved into a whirlwind of passion. All the feelings Angela had kept pent up over the past few weeks came pouring out and she wrapped her arms around his neck, surrendering to the feel of his mouth on hers.

They tumbled back onto the bed, pushing aside clothes so that they could touch bare flesh. When they both finally came up for air, Angela sighed. "Oh, that was nice. I've missed you."

Max kissed her bare shoulder. "I'm a nice guy. And I'm sorry I acted like such a jerk. I guess I do deserve to be on your Web site."

"I took you off," she said.

"You did?"

She nodded. "I don't want anyone saying anything bad about my boyfriend."

"I'm your boyfriend?"

Angela nodded. "Yes, you are officially my boyfriend."

"And since I'm your boyfriend, can I take all your clothes off now?"

She nodded again. "Yes, you may. But only if you take your clothes off, too."

"We operate so much better when we're naked, don't we."

Angela laughed, then pulled him on top of her. She wrapped her arms around his neck and kissed him hard. Fourteen years ago, she touched him for the first time and her life had changed. Maybe they were meant to be together. And maybe the fates had just been waiting for the right time.

Now that she had him, Angela didn't intend to let him go.

* * * * *

HARLEQUIN® Blaze™

COMING NEXT MONTH

Available June 29, 2010

#549 BORN ON THE 4TH OF JULY
Jill Shalvis, Rhonda Nelson, Karen Foley

#550 AMBUSHED!
Vicki Lewis Thompson
Sons of Chance

#551 THE BRADDOCK BOYS: BRENT
Kimberly Raye
Love at First Bite

#552 THE TUTOR
Hope Tarr
Blaze Historicals

#553 MY FAKE FIANCÉE
Nancy Warren
Forbidden Fantasies

#554 SIMON SAYS...
Donna Kauffman
The Wrong Bed

REQUEST YOUR FREE BOOKS!

2 FREE NOVELS
PLUS 2
FREE GIFTS!

HARLEQUIN®

Blaze™

Red-hot reads!

YES! Please send me 2 FREE Harlequin® Blaze™ novels and my 2 FREE gifts (gifts are worth about $10). After receiving them, if I don't wish to receive any more books, I can return the shipping statement marked "cancel." If I don't cancel, I will receive 6 brand-new novels every month and be billed just $4.24 per book in the U.S. or $4.71 per book in Canada. That's a saving of at least 15% off the cover price. It's quite a bargain. Shipping and handling is just 50¢ per book.* I understand that accepting the 2 free books and gifts places me under no obligation to buy anything. I can always return a shipment and cancel at any time. Even if I never buy another book, the two free books and gifts are mine to keep forever.

151/351 HDN E5LS

Name	(PLEASE PRINT)	
Address		Apt. #
City	State/Prov.	Zip/Postal Code

Signature (if under 18, a parent or guardian must sign)

Mail to the **Harlequin Reader Service:**
IN U.S.A.: P.O. Box 1867, Buffalo, NY 14240-1867
IN CANADA: P.O. Box 609, Fort Erie, Ontario L2A 5X3

Not valid for current subscribers to Harlequin Blaze books.

Want to try two free books from another line?
Call 1-800-873-8635 or visit www.morefreebooks.com.

* Terms and prices subject to change without notice. Prices do not include applicable taxes. N.Y. residents add applicable sales tax. Canadian residents will be charged applicable provincial taxes and GST. Offer not valid in Quebec. This offer is limited to one order per household. All orders subject to approval. Credit or debit balances in a customer's account(s) may be offset by any other outstanding balance owed by or to the customer. Please allow 4 to 6 weeks for delivery. Offer available while quantities last.

Your Privacy: Harlequin Books is committed to protecting your privacy. Our Privacy Policy is available online at www.eHarlequin.com or upon request from the Reader Service. From time to time we make our lists of customers available to reputable third parties who may have a product or service of interest to you. If you would prefer we not share your name and address, please check here. ☐

Help us get it right—We strive for accurate, respectful and relevant communications. To clarify or modify your communication preferences, visit us at www.ReaderService.com/consumerchoice.

HB10R

HARLEQUIN®

A Romance

FOR EVERY MOOD™

Spotlight on

Heart & Home

Heartwarming romances
where love can happen
right when you least expect it.

See the next page to enjoy a sneak peek
from Silhouette Special Edition®,
a Heart and Home series.

Introducing MCFARLANE'S PERFECT BRIDE
by USA TODAY *bestselling author Christine Rimmer,*
from Silhouette Special Edition®.

Entranced. Captivated. Enchanted.

Connor sat across the table from Tori Jones and couldn't help thinking that those words exactly described what effect the small-town schoolteacher had on him. He might as well stop trying to tell himself he wasn't interested. He was powerfully drawn to her.

Clearly, he should have dated more when he was younger.

There had been a couple of other women since Jennifer had walked out on him. But he had never been entranced. Or captivated. Or enchanted.

Until now.

He wanted her—*her,* Tori Jones, in particular. Not just someone suitably attractive and well-bred, as Jennifer had been. Not just someone sophisticated, sexually exciting and discreet, which pretty much described the two women he'd dated after his marriage crashed and burned.

It came to him that he...he *liked* this woman. And that was new to him. He liked her quick wit, her wisdom and her big heart. He liked the passion in her voice when she talked about things she believed in.

He liked *her.* And suddenly it mattered all out of proportion that she might like him, too.

Was he losing it? He couldn't help but wonder. Was he cracking under the strain—of the soured economy, the McFarlane House setbacks, his divorce, the scary changes in his son? Of the changes he'd decided he needed to make in his life and himself?

Strangely, right then, on his first date with Tori Jones, he didn't care if he just might be going over the edge. He was having a great time—having *fun,* of all things—and he didn't want it to end.

Is Connor finally able to admit his feelings to Tori, and are they reciprocated?
Find out in McFARLANE'S PERFECT BRIDE
by USA TODAY bestselling author Christine Rimmer.
Available July 2010,
only from Silhouette Special Edition®.

Bestselling Harlequin Presents® author
Penny Jordan

brings you an exciting new trilogy...

Needed:
THE WORLD'S MOST ELIGIBLE BILLIONAIRES

Three penniless sisters:
how far will they go to save the ones they love?

Lizzie, Charley and Ruby refuse to drown in their debts.
And three of the richest, most ruthless men in the world
are about to enter their lives. Pure, proud but penniless,
how far will these sisters go to save the ones they love?

Look out for

Lizzie's story—**THE WEALTHY GREEK'S
CONTRACT WIFE**, July

Charley's story—**THE ITALIAN DUKE'S
VIRGIN MISTRESS**, August

Ruby's story—**MARRIAGE: TO CLAIM HIS TWINS**,
September

www.eHarlequin.com

HP12927